W9-BNR-851

The woman was pregnant!

"Stay!" Tristan commanded his K-9 partner, and Jesse dropped down with a grunted protest.

A woman appeared in the window. Dark hair. Pale skin. Freckles. Very pregnant belly that wasn't cooperating as she struggled to crawl through the opening.

Ariel Martin. The newest teacher at Desert Valley High School. Smart. Enthusiastic. Patient. He'd heard that from more than one parent. He'd even heard it from Mia.

"You okay?" he asked, running to her side.

She shook her head, dark gray eyes wide with shock, a smear of blood on her right hand. She'd cut herself. It looked deep, but she didn't seem to notice. "There's a gunman. He tried to shoot me."

The words were calm, crisp and clear, and they chilled Tristan to the bone. Two women had already been murdered in Desert Valley. Was Ariel Martin slated to be the third?

ROOKIE K-9 UNIT:
These lawmen solve the toughest cases
with the help of their brave canine partners

Aside from her faith and her family, there's not much **Shirlee McCoy** enjoys more than a good book! When she's not teaching or chauffeuring her five kids, she can usually be found plotting her next Love Inspired Suspense story or wandering around the beautiful Inland Northwest in search of inspiration. Shirlee loves to hear from readers. If you have time, drop her a line at shirlee@shirleemccoy.com.

Books by Shirlee McCoy

Love Inspired Suspense

Rookie K-9 Unit

Secrets and Lies

Mission: Rescue

Protective Instincts
Her Christmas Guardian
Exit Strategy
Deadly Christmas Secrets
Mystery Child

Capitol K-9 Unit

Protection Detail
Capitol K-9 Unit Christmas
"Protecting Virginia"

Heroes for Hire

Running for Cover
Running Scared
Running Blind
Lone Defender
Private Eye Protector
Undercover Bodyguard
Navy SEAL Rescuer
Fugitive
Defender for Hire

Visit the Author Profile page at Harlequin.com for more titles.

SECRETS AND LIES

SHIRLEE MCCOY

H HARLEQUIN® LOVE INSPIRED® SUSPENSE

Special thanks and acknowledgment are given to Shirlee McCoy for her contribution to the Rookie K-9 Unit miniseries.

Recycling programs for this product may not exist in your area.

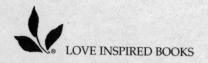

LOVE INSPIRED BOOKS

ISBN-13: 978-0-373-44758-9

Secrets and Lies

www.Harlequin.com

Printed in U.S.A.

As for God, His way is perfect; the word of the Lord is flawless. He is a shield for all who take refuge in Him.
–Psalms 18:30

To my fellow Rookie K-9 authors.
Val, Dana, Lynette, Terri and Lenora, working with the five of you was such a privilege and a pleasure! We made quite a team, and I'm so glad that I got to be part of it!

ONE

The soft buzz of her cell phone pulled Ariel Martin's attention from the ninth-grade English paper she was grading. It was good that she'd been engrossed in the essay—the student had obviously done an outstanding job. It was not so good that long shadows had drifted across the classroom floor while she was reading. It was late. Later than she'd realized.

She grabbed her phone and read the text that had come through.

Want to grab some dinner later, Ari?

"No, Easton. I do not," she muttered, shoving the phone back in her purse without responding.

Easton Riley was a nice enough guy—a math teacher who'd coached the football team to regional victory the previous year—but she wasn't interested.

She had her hands full teaching summer school, tutoring on the side, getting the classroom ready for the long-term sub who'd be taking over from mid-September through December when she had her baby. The last thing she needed or wanted was a relationship complicating things. She'd lived that for five years—always at another

person's beck and call, always worrying about what someone else wanted or needed.

She hadn't thought marriage would be that way. She'd
thought it would be a mutual effort—two people working
together to reach a common goal. She'd been wrong. She
had the divorce papers to prove it, filed in Nevada and
finalized three weeks later. Not what she'd wanted. She'd
wanted couples counseling and pastoral help. Mitch had
wanted someone else.

That had hurt. What had hurt more was how adamant
he'd been that she get rid of the baby she learned she was
carrying a week after Mitch had filed for divorce. An
abortion, that's what he'd demanded. He'd even tossed
cash at her, screaming that she'd better get rid of the kid
or he'd do it for her.

That had been the first time she'd been scared of her
ex-husband. There'd been other times after that. The fact
that he'd died in a fiery car wreck a month later should
have given her a sense of relief, but she'd felt trapped by
all the memories—good and bad—of their marriage. Las
Vegas had never been her dream. It had been Mitch's.
They'd graduated from the University of Arizona and
chased after the things he'd wanted—money, fast cars,
expensive toys. She'd been happy to go along for the ride,
because she'd loved him.

Love wasn't all it was cracked up to be.

She'd learned that the hard way, and now she was back
in her old hometown, teaching at the high school she'd
attended, trying to get ready for the daughter she'd be
raising alone.

"We'll do great, munchkin," she said, standing and
stretching a kink from her back. She glanced at the clock
that hung above the classroom door. 5:45 p.m.

Mia McKeller's brother was late. Again.

Ariel understood that the guy was busy. The Desert Valley police had had their hands full the past few months—murders, drug runners, attacks, arrests. Rumors and speculations had been running rampant through the town, and Ariel had wondered if she would have been better off staying in Vegas. At least there, she had some anonymity. There'd been no sweet old church ladies knocking on her door in the evening, handing her casseroles and asking questions about her married state, her plans for the baby, her decision to raise her daughter alone. In Desert Valley, everyone seemed to know everyone else's business. If they didn't, they wanted to know. The problem was, Ariel didn't want to explain her marriage, Mitch's death, the fact that she wasn't nearly as sorry about it as she should be. She didn't want to lie, either, so she found herself hedging around questions, giving half answers and partial truths. She preferred authenticity, but it was hard when there were so many things she couldn't or wouldn't say. Yeah. She preferred straight-up answers.

She also preferred being on time.

Something that Tristan McKeller seemed to be opposed to. At least when it came to his meetings with her.

He seemed like a nice guy. They'd spoken on the phone several times, and he'd gone out of his way to introduce himself at church. She hadn't needed the introduction. She'd seen him in town, walking with Mia and his K-9 partner. Her first thought was always that he made a handsome picture—tall and dark-haired, one hand on his sister's shoulder, the other on the dog leash. Her second was always that he really seemed to care about Mia.

And yet, he couldn't seem to make it to their meetings on time.

She grabbed her cell phone, checking to make sure she hadn't missed a call. Tristan had had to cancel two previous meetings due to his job as a K-9 officer. He'd apologized profusely, and she'd been happy to reschedule, but summer school was drawing to a close, Mia's English grade wasn't improving, and if she didn't pass, she'd wouldn't be able to join her friends in tenth grade the following year. As Mia's guardian, it was up to Tristan McKeller to ensure his sister was aware of the ramifications of her decisions to not turn in assignments, not attend class, not participate.

Of course, he'd assured Ariel that he'd been talking to Mia, working with her and trying everything he could think of to motivate his sister. Nothing was working, and they were going to have to come up with a new plan. She'd explained it all to him Sunday morning when he'd pulled her aside after church and asked if Mia's grades were improving. He'd wanted to be prepared for bad news at the meeting, he'd said, a half smile softening the hard angles of his face.

She'd noticed that.

Which had irritated her.

No more men. Ever. That was an easy enough promise to keep to herself.

Ariel sighed, grabbing the writing prompt she'd be using for Monday's composition class. She might as well get it photocopied now, because she had a feeling Tristan would be canceling again, and once she heard from him, she was going home. She had a crib to put together. The baby was due in five weeks. Plenty of time to get the nursery ready, but whenever she got started, she thought about how it was supposed to be—two people choosing colors, two people picking wall art, two people putting the crib together—and she stopped.

She couldn't keep stopping.

Babies came whether the parent was ready or not.

She walked out of the classroom, the smell of chalk dust and floor cleaner filling her nose. Desert Valley High was smaller than the Las Vegas prep school where she'd spent the first five years of her teaching career. The main hall split into two wings, and she turned to the left, by-passing the girls' restroom, the library, the cafeteria. The teacher's lounge was just ahead, the photocopy machines tucked into a cubby there.

She walked into the room, smiling at the little sign one of the teachers had hung on the refrigerator door— a smiley face with Smiles Don't Happen Here scrawled across it.

Not true, of course.

Desert Valley High was a nice place to work—good teachers, good principal, good kids, supportive parents. A dream come true, really.

If a person still had dreams.

Ariel's had all died when Mitch had thrown the cash at her and screamed that he wanted her and the baby gone from his life.

"Cut it out," she muttered, sliding the prompt into the copy machine and closing the lid. The last thing she needed to do was dwell on the past. She had an entire future to plan out and live. She also had a baby who would need her to be strong, focused and positive.

Somewhere in the school a door slammed shut, the sound faint but audible. Tristan McKeller. It had to be. The rest of the staff had gone home for the night. Ariel had been alone in the building since the head custodian, Jethro Right, had told her to lock the main doors when she left.

That was one of the nice things about being in a school this size. She had a key to the main door and could come and go as she pleased.

She left the machine and hurried into the corridor.

At least, she *tried* to hurry. The baby was gaining weight rapidly at this point, the heaviness of the pregnancy slowing Ariel down more than she'd imagined it would. She'd always been an athlete—cross-country, volleyball, soccer. She'd had to slow down the past month or so, but she still walked every day and coached the girl's track team.

By the time she reached her classroom, she was slightly out of breath, her heart racing as if she'd done the hundred-yard dash. The door was closed, no light spilling out from beneath it. Had she closed it? Had she turned off the light?

She couldn't remember doing either, and she hesitated, her hand on the doorknob, a shiver of warning working its way up her spine. There'd been moments since she'd left Las Vegas when the old fears had haunted her, when she'd found herself checking and rechecking the locks on the windows and doors of the little house she lived in. She'd found out a lot of things about Mitch after he'd died, things that had made her question herself and her ability to judge people, that had made her wonder if her entire marriage had been based on lies. According to the police, she'd been married to a criminal—a guy who'd laundered money through the casino where he'd worked, an arsonist who'd collected money after helping others commit insurance fraud. If he were alive, Mitch would be in jail.

He wasn't, and sometimes Ariel thought that the people he owed, the ones who the police said always played for keeps, might come after her to get what they were owed.

She shivered, backing away from the door. She couldn't imagine Mia's brother walking into her classroom, closing the door and turning off the light, and she really didn't think she'd done either of those things herself. She'd heard a door slam. Someone was in the school. Anyone who had any business being there would make themselves known, not wander around stealthily turning off lights.

She'd left her purse in the room, her wallet, her phone, but she could get those later. There was nothing wrong with being careful, after all. Nothing at all wrong with waiting for someone else to walk her into the room.

Heading up the corridor, she thought she heard the soft swish of a door opening behind her and turned, then saw her door swinging open, a man stepping out. Thin. Tall. Face masked by a stocking or a ski mask? He had something in his hand and raised it. A gun! She darted around the corner as a bullet slammed into the wall near her head. Plaster and cement flew into her hair, pinging off her cheek.

She didn't stop. She could hear his feet slapping against the tile, knew he'd be around the corner in heartbeat.

Run! her mind shrieked, her body clumsy with eight months of pregnancy, her legs churning in slow-motion, time speeding forward, the footsteps growing closer.

She ducked into the resource room, slamming the door closed, her hands trembling as she turned the lock. She stepped to the side just as a bullet flew through the door and smashed into a shelf of books that lined the far wall.

She had to get out!

The window was the only escape, and she ran to it, clawing at the lock mechanism. It didn't budge.

Behind her, something slammed into the door. Once. Twice. The door shook, and she knew it wouldn't be long before it flew open and the gunman appeared, weapon drawn and ready.

Please, God, please! she prayed frantically as she searched the room for another way out. There wasn't one, but an old computer monitor sat abandoned on the floor, wires tossed on top of it. She lifted it and slammed it into the window. A tiny hairline crack appeared. She slammed it again, and the glass cracked more. Behind her, the assault on the door continued, the wood starting to splinter and give.

Please, she prayed again as she lifted the monitor and threw it with all her strength.

Glass shattering.

Rookie K-9 officer Tristan McKeller heard it as he hooked his K-9 partner to a lead. The yellow lab cocked his head to the side, growling softly.

"What is it, boy?" Tristan asked, scanning the school parking lot. Only one other vehicle was parked there—a shiny black minivan that he knew belonged to Ariel Martin. He was late to their meeting. That seemed to be the story of his life this summer. Work was crazy, and his sister was crazier, and finding time to meet with Mia's summer school teacher? Nearly impossible. He'd already canceled two previous meetings. He couldn't cancel this one. Not if Mia had any hope of getting through summer school and moving on to the next grade. That's what Ariel had said when he'd pulled her aside at church last Sunday.

She can do it, Tristan. She's smart enough. We just have to find the right motivation. We'll talk about it at the meeting. You are going to be there, right?

Of course, he'd assured her that he would.

What he hadn't done was assure her that he'd be on time. A good thing, since it looked like he was going to be more than a few minutes late. Jesse was still growling, alerted to something that must have to do with the shattering glass. Kids fooling around and busting school windows? A ball tossed the wrong way, taking out a streetlight?

He hoped it was something that innocuous, but he

wasn't counting on it. Things had been happening in Desert Valley, a string of crimes that seemed to have surprised everyone in the small town. Drug runners. A dirty cop. Murder.

"Find!" he commanded, and Jesse took off, pulling against the leash in his haste to get to the corner of the building and around it. Trained in arson detection, the dog had an unerring nose for almost anything. Right now, he was on a scent, and Tristan trusted him enough to let him have his head.

Glass glittered on the pavement twenty feet away, and Jesse beelined for it, barking raucously, his tail stiff and high.

"Front!" Tristan said, and the dog returned to him, sitting impatiently, his dark eyes focused on the window.

"Stay!" Tristan commanded, and Jesse dropped down with a grunted protest. He wanted to keep going, but Tristan couldn't risk him cutting his paws on the shards of glass.

A woman appeared in the window. Dark hair. Pale skin. Freckles. Very pregnant belly that wasn't cooperating as she struggled to crawl through the opening. Ariel Martin. The newest teacher at Desert Valley High School. Smart. Enthusiastic. Patient. He'd heard that from more than one parent. He'd even heard it from Mia. The few times Tristan had spoken to Ariel, he'd been impressed by her interest in his sister, and he'd felt confident that she could help Mia regain her academic grounding. If Mia would let her.

"You okay?" he asked, running to Ariel's side.

She shook her head, dark gray eyes wide with shock, a smear of blood on her right hand. She'd cut herself. It looked deep, but she didn't seem to notice. "He's got a gun. He tried to shoot me."

The words were calm, crisp and clear, and they chilled Tristan to the bone. Two women had already been murdered in Desert Valley. Was Ariel Martin slated to be the third?

"Who?" He grabbed her arms, hauling her through the opening.

She landed on her feet, her body trembling. "I don't know. He was wearing something over his face."

"But you did see a gun?" he asked, wanting clarification before he called in a gunman on the loose.

"Saw it. Heard the bullet slam into the wall. Saw one go through the door. He was trying to get into the resource room where I was hiding, but I think he heard your dog barking and left." Her voice trembled, but she didn't hesitate, the words flowing out easily. Truth did that to people. This was no overly imaginative person freaked-out about something that *might* have been seen. This was a woman who'd been terrified by a very real, very imminent threat.

Her safety was first, but Tristan wanted to go after the guy now, before he had a chance to run. If this was connected to the other murders, this might be the break they'd been looking for. Ariel had seen the guy. Not his face. But his height, width, maybe his skin tone.

He called dispatch and asked for backup as he led Ariel to his SUV. The sooner they hunted the perp down and took him into custody, the safer everyone in the vicinity would be.

He couldn't leave the victim, though. Not until he was certain the gunman wasn't hanging around, waiting for another opportunity to strike.

"Do you think he's gone?" Ariel asked.

"Yes."

"But you don't know. Not for sure. He could be in the building somewhere, or heading around the side of the school," she responded, just a hint of a tremor in her voice. Despite her advanced pregnancy, she was fit and muscular, her legs long and slim, her arms toned. He'd noticed that the first time he'd seen her. She'd walked into church with her head high, her shoulders squared, her belly pressing against a flowy dress, and there wasn't an unattached guy in the congregation who hadn't sat up a little straighter. A few months later and her belly was bigger, but she still looked confident and determined. Being shot at could shake the toughest person, though, and it had obviously shaken her.

He opened the passenger door, helped her into the seat.

"I do know for sure," he assured her. "Or at least, Jesse does." He pointed to his K-9 partner. The dog was relaxed, his tail wagging, his scruff down. He'd be growling or barking if he sensed danger. Instead, he'd loped back to their vehicle, not even a hint of tension in his muscular body.

Good, but not good enough for Tristan. He wanted to search the school, make sure the guy hadn't left anything behind—firearms, bombs, some kind of accelerant that he could use at a later date to cause mass casualties. Not likely, but it was always better to be safe than sorry.

Same for Ariel. Aside from her paleness and the cut on her hand, she seemed to be doing okay. It was better to get her checked out at the hospital, though, and make certain there wouldn't be any complications with her pregnancy. He called dispatch with the request for an ambulance as he opened the back of the SUV and pulled out a first-aid kit.

"I don't need an ambulance," Ariel protested.

He ignored her, pulling on disposable gloves and lifting her wounded hand. "This is deep. You'll need stitches."

He pressed gauze to the wound, and she winced.

"Sorry." He didn't ease up on the pressure, though. She'd bled a lot. Probably more than she realized.

"It's fine." Her free hand lay against her belly. No ring on that one or the one he was holding. He knew she was a widow. He'd heard rumors that her husband had died shortly after she'd found out she was pregnant. He hadn't asked for details, but he'd wondered. Mia really liked Ariel, and Tristan figured it took a special kind of person to win his sister's affection. He'd imagined that Ariel must be gentle, quiet, maybe a little sentimental, but taking off her wedding ring so soon after her husband's death didn't seem sentimental at all.

Then again, maybe it was. He didn't know much about those kinds of things, and he didn't know Ariel well enough to ask. What he did know was that she deserved better than this.

He met her eyes, saw fear in the depth of her dark gray gaze.

"It's going to be okay," he said.

"I hope so."

"It will be. The ambulance should be here soon. They'll triage this before they transport you," he said, and she frowned.

"Like I said, I don't need an ambulance."

"You're nine months pregnant—"

"Eight, and—"

Whatever she planned to say was cut off by a police cruiser's siren. The vehicle screamed into the parking lot, lights flashing, tires shrieking as Eddie Harmon's car squealed to a stop beside Tristan.

Eddie jumped out of the car, his uniform shirt pulled tight across his stomach, his shoes scuffed and pants wrinkled.

"What's going on here? Got a call about a gunman?"

He eyed Ariel, taking in her bleeding hand and her very pregnant belly. "I'm assuming it was a false alarm, maybe a misunderstanding?"

Of course he'd assume that. Eddie liked to take the easy route to police work. His focus was on his family and his upcoming retirement rather than his job. He wasn't a bad cop, but he wasn't a good one, either.

Tristan would have preferred to have one of the K-9 officers there. He trusted Eddie to do his job, but he hated to leave Ariel with a guy who probably wasn't going to take her seriously. She looked too pale, too vulnerable, and he was tempted to stay right where he was until the rest of the K-9 team arrived. But, every minute he waited was another minute the perp had to escape.

"There *was* a shooter," Tristan assured him. "I'm going to take Jesse into the building and secure the scene. There's an ambulance on the way. Can you stay with the victim until it arrives? Until we know what the perp is after, we can't assume he's not going to try to strike again."

"In other words, you want me to take guard duty," Eddie said, crossing his arms over his belly and eyeing Tristan dispassionately.

"Right."

"I guess I can do that." Eddie shrugged. "Easier than walking around the building looking for the perp."

That's exactly what Tristan figured he'd say.

He met Ariel's eyes. She still looked scared. She also looked exhausted, her face pale, her cheekbones gaunt. He hadn't noticed that before, but then he'd been telling himself for months that he shouldn't be noticing anything about Mia's teacher. His life was filled up with work and with his sister. He didn't have time for relationships. Especially not complicated ones. A pregnant widow? That was way more than he had room for in his life.

"This might take a while. When I finish, I'll check back in with you."

She nodded, and he called Jesse to heel and jogged to the building. The perp hadn't gone out the front. Jesse would have scented him when they'd walked back to the SUV.

"Where is he?" Tristan asked, and Jesse's ears perked, his nose going to the air and then the ground. Tristan would have preferred to have Shane Weston and his apprehension dog, Bella, there tracking the perp, but waiting was out of the question.

"Find him!" he urged, and Jesse ran to the back of the school, nosing the cement path that led to double-wide doors. They yawned open, the corridor beyond silent and empty. This had to have been the entrance point. The exit point, too, if the guy was gone.

Tristan followed the dog across the threshold, calling out as he entered the building, warning that police were present. No response. He hadn't expected one. He really didn't expect the perp to have hung around.

Jesse tugged him through the hall, passing classroom after classroom. The lab stopped at room 119, sniffing the floor before walking inside. There, he nosed around near a teacher's desk, sniffing a dark blue sweater that hung over the back of a chair. He huffed quietly and left it, continuing across the room to a storage closet that stood open.

Had the guy been in the closet? Maybe waiting for Ariel to return to the classroom? The thought turned Tristan's stomach. Master police dog trainer Veronica Earnshaw had been murdered in her place of employment, shot to death while microchipping a new litter of puppies for the Canyon County K-9 Training Center. Since then,

Desert Valley had been on edge. That wasn't the first murder in the area. Five years ago, K-9 officer Ryder Hayes had lost his wife on the night of the annual Desert Valley Police Department dance and fund-raiser. She'd been shot and killed while carrying her dress home just hours before the party.

The perp had shot at Ariel. Was this newest incident somehow related to the other two?

Jesse left the closet, tracing a path from there back to the desk and then out into the hallway. They moved through the dimly lit corridor, the dusky sunlight barely penetrating this far into the building. They reached the corner where the east and west wings jutted to either side of the main building, and Jesse barked, prancing around what looked like bits of concrete and wallboard.

"Front!" Tristan commanded, and the dog returned, dropping down on his haunches.

"Stay!" he said, motioning for the dog to lie on the floor, then moving past and looking at the debris that littered the gray-white tiles. A chunk of wall had been blown from the corner, the bullet still lodged in concrete. Tristan called for Jesse and continued on past several closed doors. He didn't need the dog to show him where Ariel had been hiding. The door to the room had been shot through, the old wood caving in from the force of a foot kicked into it over and over again. Another few well-placed kicks and the door would have caved in, giving the gunman a clear shot at his intended victim.

A random act of violence?

Tristan didn't think so. Everything about this seemed premeditated—the perp hiding in the closet, the mask that had hidden his features, the determination to get through a locked door. The guy had been after blood, and if Tristan hadn't had a meeting scheduled with Ariel, he might have gotten it.

God always has a way.

It's what his father had told him over and over again. It's what Tristan's mother had repeated during Tristan's challenging teenage years. Since they'd died, Tristan had been too busy trying to raise Mia to spend much time trying to figure out what God's way was.

Maybe that had been his mistake. Maybe it was the reason why Mia was struggling so much in school and with making friends. Becoming a K-9 police officer had seemed like the perfect transition from being an army dog handler into civilian life, but that wasn't the reason Tristan had signed on to the Canyon County K-9 Center Training Course. He'd joined in honor of his army buddy and good friend Mike Riverton who'd died the previous May.

Mike had sung the praises of the K-9 program, and he'd been trying to get Tristan to apply. Then Mike had died—killed when he'd fallen down steep stairs at his home. That's the story Tristan had been told, and that's what the medical examiner's records said, but Tristan wasn't buying it. A guy like Mike—trained in mountain climbing and free-climbing rock walls—would never have fallen and not been able to catch himself.

Yeah. Things around Desert Valley weren't what they'd seemed when Tristan had moved there for the program. Small towns, he was learning, often hid big secrets.

He frowned, his thoughts going back to Ariel, the way she'd looked when she'd been struggling to escape through the broken window, the fear in her eyes, the subtle trembling of her voice.

Sometimes, small towns also hid murderers.

Not for long, though.

Tristan knew the Desert Valley PD was closing in on

the killer. He was certain it was just a matter of time before the perpetrator was found. But, time wasn't anyone's friend when a murderer was on the loose.

A murderer, he thought, eyeing the splintered door and the bullet hole, *who might have just attempted to strike again.*

TWO

She'd almost died.

Ariel couldn't shake the thought, and she couldn't ignore it as an EMT leaned over her cut palm, eyeing the still-bleeding wound.

"You're going to need stitches," the young woman said brusquely. "We can transport you to the hospital for that, or you can go to the clinic. Your call."

"I'll go to the clinic," Ariel responded by rote.

If she'd died, the baby would have died. Thinking about that was worse than thinking about herself, broken and bleeding on the floor of the resource room.

She shuddered, and the EMT frowned.

"Are you sure?" she asked, her tone a little gentler. "You seem shaky, and they could check on the baby. It might give you a little peace of mind."

Aside from the guy who'd shot at her being thrown in jail, there wasn't much of anything that could give her that. "I'm sure."

The woman nodded, pressing thick gauze to the wound and wrapping it with a tight layer of surgical tape. "That should hold it until you get to the clinic. Have someone drive you. Husband, family."

"All right." Except that Ariel didn't have a husband and

she didn't have any family. She was making new friends at church and at work, but even after five months, they weren't the kind of relationships she could count on in a pinch.

If the principal came to check out the damage to the school, she'd probably offer to give Ariel a ride. Pamela Moore's daughter, Regina, had been Ariel's best friend from kindergarten through their sophomore year of high school. They'd stayed close after Ariel had moved away, and when Regina had taken her dream job working as NICU nurse in Phoenix, Ariel had cheered her on.

Regina had been the reason Ariel had been offered the job in Desert Valley. She'd contacted her mother, pleaded Ariel's case and gotten her an interview for a job that had opened up when another teacher had gotten married and left town.

It had seemed like a God-thing, the opportunity coming out of left field at a time when Ariel had been desperate to get away from Las Vegas and all the memories it held. She'd wanted a quiet little town to raise her daughter in. She'd wanted a safe environment where everyone knew everyone and where small crimes were considered a big deal. She'd thought that was what Desert Valley offered, all her sweet childhood memories leading her to believe the place would be perfect. Now, she wasn't so sure.

Several Desert Valley police vehicles had pulled into the parking lot and K-9 teams were spread out across the school grounds. Ariel could see a female officer walking through the gym field, her long hair pulled back in a ponytail, a golden retriever trotting in front of her. Ellen Foxcroft. A nice young woman who everyone in town seemed to like. Her mother was a different story. Marian Foxcroft was notorious for sticking her nose in where it didn't belong. She had money and influence in Desert

Valley, and she wasn't afraid to throw both around to get what she wanted.

Unfortunately she also had enemies. She'd been attacked a few months ago and left in a coma. It was one of the many crimes that had been taking up the front page of the town's newspaper.

Ariel had tried not to pay much attention to the stories. She had enough stress and worry in her life. She hadn't wanted to add to it, and she'd been afraid...so afraid that she'd made another mistake—just like the one she'd made when she'd married Mitch.

She touched her stomach, feeling almost guilty for the thought.

"Ma'am?" the EMT said. "Would you like me to call someone for you?"

"No. I'm fine." She stood on wobbly legs and moved past the EMT just to prove that she could. Her keys were in her classroom. So were her purse and her cell phone. The house she'd bought with money her great-aunt had left her a decade ago was only two miles from the school, but walking there wasn't an option. Not with the gunman still out there somewhere.

Had Tristan found any sign of the guy in the school? Was he okay? She'd watched him walk toward the building, and she'd wanted to caution him to be careful, because the gunman had meant business. He'd been bent on murder, and if Ariel had walked into her classroom, she'd have probably been shot before she'd even realized she was a target.

She shivered, rubbing her arms against the chill that just wouldn't seem to leave her.

"You holding up okay?" someone asked.

She turned and found herself looking into Tristan McKeller's dark brown eyes.

"I was just thinking about you," she said, the words escaping before she realized how they'd sound. "What I mean—"

"Is that you were wondering if I'd found the gunman?" he offered, and she nodded.

"Yes. And if you were okay. Apparently, you are."

"I am, but the gunman is still on the loose. We've got a couple of K-9 teams trying to track him. Hopefully, we'll have him in custody soon. You said he was wearing some sort of mask?"

"It seemed like it. I only got a glimpse as he was coming out of my room."

"Were you heading there when you noticed him?"

"I was on my way back from the Xerox machine. I'd heard a door slamming shut, and I thought it was you." She spoke quickly, filling him in on the details and doing everything in her power to not allow emotion to seep into her voice. Breaking down in front of people wasn't something she liked to do. Even when Mitch had screamed at her, telling her that the baby she was carrying would ruin his life, she hadn't cried.

She finished and Tristan nodded. "Matches with what I saw. There's a bullet slug in the corner of the wall and one through the door into the room where you were hiding. If you'd been standing in front of the door—"

"I made sure that I wasn't." She cut him off. She didn't want to speculate, she didn't want to imagine. She'd been spared. Her baby had been spared.

God looking out for them?

She wanted to believe that.

She'd been trying hard to believe that everything that had happened—all the difficulty and trouble—would turn out for the good. There were days, though, when she questioned His goodness, wondered if He'd decided to turn His face away from her.

"Smart thinking, Ariel. It saved your life." His gaze dropped to her stomach, to the baby bump that pulled her silky summer top taut over her abdomen. "And your baby's. I guess you decided against the ambulance ride?"

"I'll get stitches at the clinic." Maybe. Or maybe she'd use a couple of butterfly bandages and hope for the best. The last thing she wanted was to walk out of the local medical clinic alone after dark, and there was no way she was going to ask Principal Moore to go with her. Not when the gunman was still on the loose. What if he came after Ariel again? What if someone else was in the line of fire?

The thought made her stomach churn.

"You're new to town," Tristan said, the comment taking her by surprise.

"I've been here for a few months, and I lived here when I was a kid," she corrected, not quite sure where he was going with the conversation.

"You were in Las Vegas prior to your move?"

"Yes."

"And your husband—"

"He was my ex, and he died a few weeks before I accepted the job offer here."

His expression softened, as if he realized there was a lot more to her story than anyone in town knew. "Had you been divorced long?"

"I'm not sure what that has to do with anything."

"Most violent crimes aren't committed by strangers. Most involve people who know each other. Is there a new relationship? A boyfriend? Ex-boyfriend? Someone who might be holding grudge?"

"Do I look like I have time for another relationship?" she asked with a laugh that she knew sounded bitter and hard.

She swallowed down the emotion, tried again. "There's no one else. My ex-husband died three weeks after our divorce was finalized."

"Can I ask the cause of death?"

"A car accident. He drove off a hillside and crashed into a tree. The car burst into flames on impact."

"I'm sorry."

"Me, too. He wasn't a very nice guy, but no one deserves that."

He studied her for a moment, his eyes such a dark brown the irises were nearly invisible. They reminded her of Mia's, the lashes black and thick. Mia, though, always looked sullen. Tristan looked concerned.

"I'm sorry," he repeated, and she tensed, not comfortable with the pity she saw in his eyes.

She didn't need anyone to feel sorry for her. She just needed to move on with her life, make a safe home for her baby and create something out of the nothing she'd been left with when Mitch had told her they were done.

"Like I said, so am I, but there's nothing I can do to change it. All I can do is make a good life for our child." *My* child was what she'd wanted to say, but Mitch would always be part of their little girl's life, the shadowy parent who existed as nothing more than a name, a photograph, a hole in the heart.

"It's still tough, Ariel. There isn't a woman on the planet who doesn't deserve better than what you got. It's getting late, and you need to get those stitches. How about I follow you over to the clinic? Jesse and I can escort you in and then follow you home when you're done." He touched his dog's head, and the yellow lab seemed to smile, its tongue lolling out.

"I—"

"You know it's the safest thing, right? Until we find

out who this guy is and why he took a shot at you, you need to be cautious."

She knew. She didn't like it, but she knew.

"All right," she conceded. "But I'd rather just go home. A couple of butterfly bandages will take care of this."

Tristan didn't agree with the butterfly bandage idea, but he wasn't going to argue. Ariel knew what she wanted and after being married to a *not very nice* guy, she probably didn't need anyone telling her what decisions to make.

"That's fine. I'll walk you into the school. You can get your things and then we'll head out."

"You aren't needed here?" she asked as they headed across the parking lot.

"I was off duty when I arrived. The chief assigned the case to someone else."

"It's probably for the best," she said, brushing a few strands of hair from her cheek, the bandage on her hand crisp white in the fading light.

"Why do you say that?" He led her through the front door and into a wide lobby. Posters hung from walls, announcing clubs that would be meeting again in the fall.

"Mia," she responded. That was it. No other explanation.

"You think I should be spending more time with her?" He tried to keep defensiveness out of his voice, but he was feeling it just the way he did every time some well-meaning neighbor or church lady or school counselor pointed out that Mia needed more attention and time than what he was able to provide.

"I have no idea how much time you spend with her. I just know it can't be easy raising a teenager. Especially one who's been through a really difficult loss."

She was right about that.

He'd been an only child until he was seventeen, and he knew nothing about kids or teenage girls. He was learning, but it was a slow process. One that Mia didn't seem to have much patience for. "Mia has been through a lot. The last couple of years have been hard on both of us."

"I know, and I have a lot of sympathy for both of you, but hard times aren't an excuse for poor work." She stopped short and looked straight into his eyes. He was struck by that—by the directness of her gaze, the unapologetic way she pointed out the truth.

"I've told her that a dozen times."

"Probably a dozen too many. Kids like Mia need structure. They need consequences, too."

"I hope you're not talking about me letting her fail, because I'm not willing to do that."

"If she doesn't improve her grade in my class, she's going to fail, and there's nothing either of us can do about it." She sighed and started walking again. "I was thinking more along the lines of grounding her until her grades come up."

"I've done that. I've also made her come to work with me on her days off, so that I can make sure she's not goofing off. None of it seems to matter. She still turns in shoddy assignments."

"When she turns them in at all," Ariel added, and he couldn't argue the point. Mia had received zeros on her last three assignments.

"I've been thinking about hiring a tutor to work with her. She hates the idea." It was the only option they hadn't explored. He could hire someone, see if that person could help nudge Mia into focusing on school again. "She's a smart kid. Before my parents died, she was in the gifted program."

"I know. I saw her records. Her standardized test scores

are high, too." She stopped at the yellow police tape that blocked off one corridor of the school. "Tutoring will help, but she needs to know that people are invested in her life."

"She's got plenty of people invested. She just isn't appreciative of the fact," he muttered.

"Fourteen-year-olds seldom are." She smiled, but her gaze was focused on the hallway beyond the tape. "I guess I should get my things," she said quietly.

"I can get them for you," he offered. "If you'd rather not go back to the classroom."

"I'll have to go back Monday, so I may as well face it now." She lifted the police tape and shimmied under it, her advanced pregnancy not seeming to hinder her movements.

Up ahead, rookie K-9 officer James Harrison and his bloodhound, Hawk, crisscrossed the hallway, moving from side to side and back again.

"We're moving through," Tristan said, and James gave a brief nod, his focus on a wadded-up piece of paper that lay on the glossy tile.

"Anything interesting?" Tristan asked, and James finally looked up.

"I'm not sure. Hawk alerted here, so I'm going to process it like it is. It could have just been left behind by a kid and kicked by the gunman when he ran through." He shrugged, his gaze shifting to Ariel. "We'll figure it out though, and get this guy behind bars as quickly as possible."

He was trying to reassure her, but Ariel didn't look convinced. She looked tense, her arms crossed protectively over her stomach, her bandaged hand resting on the swell of her abdomen.

"I appreciate that," she said. "I'll feel a lot safer when he's in custody."

"Do you have any idea who it was?" James asked, opening up an evidence collection kit. He took a quick photo of the paper, then put on gloves and lifted it.

"No, but I don't think he's anyone I know."

"You didn't see his face?" James carefully opened the sheet, studying words that were scrawled across it.

"No. He was wearing a mask of some sort. I already explained everything to Officer McKeller."

"I know it's frustrating, but you'll probably be explaining things to a lot of people, Ms. Martin," James responded. "Unfortunately, that's the way these cases usually work. Lots of questions asked over and over again. Did the chief give you permission to leave the scene?"

"She's been cleared to go," Tristan responded. "I'm going to escort her and make sure she arrives home safely. At this point, that's my top priority."

She tensed at his words, but she didn't protest them.

"Good," James said. "If the guy was planning this, if he found out information to help him achieve his goal, there's no guarantee he won't go after her somewhere else." He held up the paper, so that Tristan could read the handwritten words.

Desert Valley High School
Room 119
Ariel Martin

They were scrawled in black ink, every *i* dotted with a circle. The *A* underlined.

Ariel took a step back, her gaze focused on the paper, her face leeched of color. Freckles dotted her nose and her cheeks, giving the impression of youth, but there was maturity in her eyes—a deep knowledge of what it meant to struggle, to suffer and to survive.

She'd been through a lot. Now she was going through more. That bothered him. It made him want to do everything in his power to keep her safe.

"Are you okay?" he asked, and she nodded.

"Yes. I..." She pressed her lips together, sealing in whatever she'd planned to say. "You'll think I'm nuts."

"There are a lot worse things that people can be," he responded, and she smiled, a dimple flashing in her right cheek. She had a pretty smile, a soft one.

"True. The thing about the letter...the writing looks really familiar."

"A student?" James suggested.

"No. My ex-husband."

"Did you part on good terms?" James asked. "Is it possible—?"

"He's dead." Tristan cut in. There was no sense walking down that road. A dead man didn't write notes. He didn't carry a gun. He didn't stalk his ex.

"That blows a hole in my theory, then," James responded, carefully placing the note in an evidence bag.

"What about the writing made you think of your ex?" Tristan asked Ariel.

"Mitch always underlined the *A* in my name, and he always used circles to dot *i*'s."

"That's information anyone could have known," he pointed out. "Friends, coworker, family. Most would have seen his writing at one point or another."

"He didn't have family. It was one of the things that brought us together. Two college students with no one." She blushed, shook her head. "It's an old story, and there's no reason to tell it now. I can get you a list of Mitch's associates, but I can't guarantee that I know all of them. He was involved in some things I didn't know about until after he died."

"Affairs?" James asked bluntly, and Ariel shrugged.

"I found that out before we divorced. After he died, the police started questioning me about other things. He'd been involved in a money laundering scheme in Las Vegas and insurance fraud in Nevada and several other states. If he'd lived, he'd have been arrested." She said it as if it didn't matter, her face and voice devoid of emotion. It had to have hurt, though. It had to have made her doubt all the things she'd thought were true about herself and her relationships.

"I'm sorry, Ariel," Tristan said, and she offered him that same soft pretty smile.

"So you keep saying. Sorry doesn't change things, though, and it's not going to help you figure out who tried to shoot me. I'm not familiar with any of the people who were involved in criminal activities with Mitch, but I can print out a list of his work associates and friends and swing it by the police department tomorrow. I may have a sample of his writing, too. If that will help."

"It will," Tristan said. "I'll talk to Chief Jones and see if we can send the paper for handwriting analysis. The state crime lab should be able to process it."

"You want me to handle that while you escort her home?" James asked.

Tristan met Ariel's eyes. She didn't look any less tired than she had a few minutes ago, and he thought she needed to be home more than she needed to wait around the crime scene while he did something another officer could handle. "Sure."

"Okay," James said. "Come on, Hawk, let's see what else we can find."

The bloodhound offered a quick bark in response and moved down the hall, ears brushing the ground as he moved.

Ariel must have taken that as her cue to leave. She headed down the hall, moving toward her room at a half run that Tristan didn't think could be good for her or the baby.

But, then, what did he know?

He'd never spent much time around pregnant women. He didn't know what the protocol was for exercise this late in a pregnancy. She was in good health and very fit. If she wanted to jog, who was he to question her? If she wanted to run away from her problems, who was he to tell her it couldn't be done?

Obviously, the discussion about her ex had been painful. It was just as obvious that she was done talking about it.

That was fine.

For now.

He kept silent as he followed her to her room. She stopped at the yellow crime-scene tape that blocked her path. Fingerprint powder coated the doorknob and the edge of the door. More dusted the wall.

"This isn't going to be fun on Monday," Ariel murmured.

"We'll have things processed and cleaned up by then." He lifted the tape, and she walked across the threshold and straight to her desk. She grabbed her sweater, opened a drawer and took out her purse.

"You want to check to make sure everything is there?" he asked, and she opened the purse, pulling out a cell phone and a wallet.

"Credit card. Debit card. Cash." She listed the items one at a time as she looked through the wallet. "Everything is here."

"Keys?"

She lifted a key ring. "Here."

"Anything else you want to grab? You may not be able to get in here tomorrow."

"I can access lesson plans and grades online. I have what I need." She slid into the sweater, then hitched the purse onto her shoulder. Nothing about her was fancy or overdone. Very little makeup, hair pulled into a ponytail, clothes understated. Her emotions were understated, too. No panic or tears or frantic speculating. She seemed determined to hold herself together.

That was good. It was easier to get information from people who were clearheaded. Tristan might not be working her case, but he could pick her brain, see if the ex-husband who'd died might be the key to the attack. One thing he couldn't do was walk away and not worry about the case or Ariel. He couldn't know for sure, but he thought that Ariel might have come to Desert Valley to escape her past and to try to create a more peaceful future. He wanted to make sure she was able to do both. He also wanted to know if the attack against her was personal.

There was a big part of him hoping that this newest trouble wasn't related to the other crimes that had happened in town. Desert Valley PD was under pressure to solve two murders and investigate two suspicious deaths. Plus there was the attack on Marian Foxcroft, which had to be related. They'd been hunting for a killer for months and still had no suspect.

If Ariel's shooter proved to be connected, they might have to shift their focus, stop looking for an opportunistic murderer and start looking for a serial killer.

THREE

Ariel wouldn't fall apart.

She absolutely refused to.

And not just because Tristan was beside her, his dark gaze focused on her, his eyes filled with concern and compassion.

No. She wouldn't fall apart, because if she did, she wasn't sure she'd ever pull herself back together again.

Legs trembling, heart racing, she still managed to walk out of the school and make her way toward the minivan she'd purchased a week after the divorce was finalized. Mitch had wanted the Jaguar, and she'd been happy to give it to him. She'd still had plenty in her savings account, all the money from her great-aunt's estate that Ariel had refused to allow Mitch to spend on trips or expensive toys because she'd wanted to buy a house one day. It didn't have to be big. Just cute and cozy with a nice fenced yard.

How many times had Mitch laughed at that dream? Told her that high-rise condo living in the city limits was more their style?

More *his* style, but she'd never said that, because she'd loved him and she'd wanted him to be happy. Plus, there'd been a part of her that had thought that eventually he'd get tired of the fast-paced, high-flying lifestyle and settle into the kind of pedestrian family life Ariel remembered from childhood. Before her parents had died, she'd had the pretty little house, the big yard, the fresh-baked cookies when she got home from school. At least, she thought she'd had it. She'd visited the house when she'd moved back to Desert Valley and realized it wasn't nearly as pretty as she'd remembered it, the yard not as spacious. That hadn't bothered her. She still cherished the memories she had of her time in the house, but she also realized they'd been made even more beautiful by the time that had passed since she'd been there.

Time changed memories and tricked the mind. Sometimes it made the past into what a person wanted it to be. Sometimes it made connections that weren't really there. Was that what had happened with the handwriting on the piece of paper? Had it only seemed to be like Mitch's writing because Ariel had been terrified, the memories of Mitch's last words to her, still haunting her mind and her dreams?

"Get rid of the baby or I'll do it for you!"

An idle threat is what she'd thought, words meant to manipulate her into giving him what he wanted—freedom from her, from every obligation and burden that marriage and family brought.

She'd despised him for that for way too long, wasting weeks fuming over what he'd asked her to do, and then he'd died, and she'd had nothing to do with her anger but let it go.

So, maybe all those pent-up memories and emotions had made her see what wasn't on the piece of paper. Maybe the writing had been nothing more than a note scribbled by a student who'd needed to find her class.

She fished her keys out of her purse, unlocking the minivan as she reached it. She could feel Tristan stand-

ing behind her, his presence both disconcerting and comforting.

"I'll follow you to your place," he said as she climbed
into the vehicle.

She wanted to tell him not to bother. Not because she
didn't appreciate the offer, but because she didn't want
to start needing someone again.

Isn't that why she'd been with Mitch? Because she'd
been alone in the world, and she'd needed someone to
connect with, someone to call family?

Look how well that had worked out.

She'd ended up married and alone. Then, she'd ended
up divorced and alone. Now, she was alone and in trouble. It would be nice to rely on someone else. Especially
when her entire life seemed to be falling to pieces. But,
needing someone left a person vulnerable. She'd learned
that lesson a little too late to save herself from heartache,
but she'd learned it well.

She wouldn't make the mistake again.

On the other hand, she wasn't foolish enough to think
she didn't need protection. With a gunman on the loose,
his motive unclear, she couldn't turn down Tristan's offer.

She was too afraid.

"Sounds good," she said, fumbling with her seat belt,
because she didn't want to look into Tristan's eyes again.
There was something unsettling about him, about the way
that he looked at her, the way he really seemed to see her.

"Let me," he offered, taking the belt from her clumsy
bandaged hand and reaching over her stomach. He
snapped it into place easily and moved back quickly, but
for some reason, her cheeks heated, her face flushing a
dozen shades of red.

"When you get to the house, stay in the van until I
check out your property, okay?" He closed the door before

she could respond, jogging to an SUV and opening the back hatch for his dog. Jesse jumped in, the lab's golden fur nearly white in the evening light.

It took a couple of seconds for Ariel to realize she needed to start the van and a couple more to actually do it. By the time she drove out of the parking lot, her cheeks had cooled.

Delayed reaction from the attack. That's what she told herself as Tristan's SUV pulled onto the road behind her.

She wasn't sure she believed it.

Night would fall soon, blackness shrouding the quiet street where Ariel lived. She'd chosen the location purposely—close to school and the town's business district, but far enough away that she could have the solitude she needed. The house had been on the market for a while. A fixer-upper that no one had wanted to put the time and money into, the two-story farmhouse stood on a double lot that backed to a wide swath of open land. She'd purchased the place well under market value, and she'd been spending most of her free time getting it ready for the baby.

Mitch would have laughed at the idea, but she'd known she could make the old house into a comfortable home. Eventually, she'd invite people over, do a little entertaining, get back into the swing of being the person she'd once been.

She pulled into her driveway, Tristan right on her bumper.

He was out of his SUV before she could open her door, motioning for her to stay where she was as he attached Jesse's lead. The dog jumped from the back of the SUV, his blond tail wagging, his face set in what looked like wide-mouthed grin. He looked like most of the yellow labs she'd seen—stocky body, broad head, short coat. He was fitter, though, his lean body made for the work he did. In other circumstances, Ariel would have been amused by the perpetually happy dog. Right then, all she wanted was to get into her house, close all the shades and hide from the world.

Tristan made a sweep of the yard, walking Jesse along the perimeter and then to the front door. Finally, he seemed satisfied and jogged to the van.

"Ready?" he asked, opening the door and offering her a hand out.

"Not really," she responded, the honest answer slipping out as he walked her up the porch stairs. An old swing hung from the eaves, the metal chains creaking as she unlocked the door. Across the street, Edna Wilkinson's porch light went on. She'd probably noticed the strange SUV in Ariel's driveway and wanted to get a better look.

"You're scared," Tristan said as she led the way into the house.

"I'd be foolish not to be." She turned to face him, was surprised at how tall he suddenly seemed. At least eight inches taller than her, and she wasn't short. "Someone nearly killed me. That's not something I can put on the back burner and worry about later."

"You're right, and I can assure you that the Desert Valley police are taking this seriously."

"They take every case seriously, don't they? Look at what they've accomplished these past few months. Cracking down on that extortion ring and putting corrupt police officer Ken Bucks behind bars. Finding the bank heist money that was hidden outside town."

"Yes," Tristan responded. "Sometimes, though, it helps to be reminded that you're not alone in your struggles."

The words echoed the thought she'd had at the school— the one about being alone and in trouble—and her cheeks heated again. "Yes. I guess it does. Thanks for escorting me home, Tristan. I appreciate it."

"It sounds like you're kicking me out."

"Just giving you the freedom to go back to whatever you were doing before you saved my life."

"I was heading for a meeting with you," he reminded her, a smile in his eyes.

She couldn't help it. She smiled in return, some of the tension she'd been feeling slipping away. "I'd forgotten all about that."

"Tell you what, how about I take a look at the locks on your doors while I'm here? Make sure they're strong enough to keep someone out? Then, we can discuss my obnoxious sister and her academic troubles."

"She's not obnoxious."

"Much?" he asked, and she laughed.

"That's better," he commented, as he fiddled with the bolt on the front door.

"What's better?"

"You don't look like you're going to shatter anymore. This bolt looks good. Let's look at the back door." He said it all so quickly that the first few words almost didn't register.

By the time they did, he was halfway down the hall, heading to the back of the house.

"I wasn't going to shatter," she muttered, hurrying after him.

"I didn't say you were. I just said you looked like you might." He'd reached the mudroom and the door that opened from it into the backyard.

"I'm not the kind of person who shatters when things don't go her way," she replied, but he was turning the lock, frowning at the door, and she wasn't sure he heard.

"This could be a lot stronger, Ariel," he finally said.

"I can have it replaced."

"You could also put a door between the mudroom and the kitchen." He touched the doorjamb that had once housed an interior door. Someone had taken it down before Ariel had bought the property.

"I think the one that goes there is out in the shed behind the house. I found it there after I moved in."

"I've got the day off tomorrow. How about I stop by and hang it for you? Two layers of defense are better than one."

"I can do it." Probably. Although, lately the pregnancy was making her tired. The further along she got, the more difficult everyday tasks became. She tried not to dwell on that. She tried not to think about how much more difficult it would be to parent alone than it would have been to parent as a team.

"Just because you can do it, doesn't mean you have to. If you don't want to accept the help as a gift, you can point me in the direction of a good tutor for Mia and give me a pass on being late to our meeting today. I did miss… what? Two previous meetings?"

"You also saved my life, so you've already earned the pass on that, but…" She hesitated, not sure about the offer she was about to make. She liked Mia. The teen had a great vocabulary and a flair for words. She also had a chip on her shoulder and an attitude to go with it. "I've been doing some tutoring on the side, working with some of the local kids getting them ready for SAT and ACT tests. I'd love to work with Mia."

"I couldn't ask you to do that."

"I offered. Just like you offered to put up my door. Bring her over tomorrow. While you're fixing the door, I'll help her with the paper that's due Monday."

"She has a paper due Monday?"

"Yes, and two extra credit assignments due by Friday. If she doesn't get As, she's not going to pass my class."

"It would devastate Mia to be held back a year."

"I know. If I could make an exception, I would. I can't."

"I wouldn't ask you to. She needs to pass on her own merit. It's not like she's not capable of it." He ran a hand over his hair, rubbed the back of his neck. He looked exasperated and worried. Like any parent would be if his child were failing. Only Mia wasn't his child. She was his sister. That had to be complicating the dynamics between them.

"Were you and Mia close before your parents passed away?" she asked, and regretted the question immediately. It was too personal, something that he might discuss with a counselor. Not his sister's teacher.

"I joined the military when I was eighteen. Mia was one. I guess you could say we barely knew each other before I became her guardian. I saw her during my leave, but that wasn't enough to create the kind of bond that would make this situation easier."

"I guess it's my turn to say I'm sorry," she said, her heart aching for what they'd both lost.

"It's been hard, but we're doing okay, slowly getting to know each other better. I think we'll both survive her teenage years."

"Think?"

He laughed, the warmth of it ringing through the quiet house. "I should have said 'survive with our sanity intact.' Now, how about we stop talking about my sister and finish looking at your locks?"

He walked to a window, frowning at the wood pane and old fashioned lock. "It would be very easy for someone to break the lock and climb in the window."

"That's a cheerful thought," she muttered, her heart

thrumming at the thought of a masked intruder entering the house while she slept.

"What's through here?" He pushed open pocket doors that led into the office. There'd been a desk there when she'd moved in—an old rolltop that still stood against the wall. Light from the hallway filtered in, but she'd closed the shades earlier, and the room seemed dark and dreary.

She flicked on the light, waiting as Tristan checked a front window. It was newer than the one in the parlor, but he still didn't seem happy. "Definitely need some updating here. How about we do this—I'll work on getting the house more secure while you work on helping my sister pass ninth-grade English?"

It was a decent deal, but she didn't want to become fodder for the town rumor mill. If Edna saw Tristan hanging around, she'd spread the news lightning fast. Before anyone even asked for the truth, the entire town would think that she and Tristan were dating.

"I—"

Jesse growled, the hair on the scruff of his neck standing up as he moved toward the window, nosed the shade. He didn't look happy anymore. He looked ready to attack.

Tristan took Ariel's arm, nudging her into the hall. "Wait here."

"What—?"

"Stay here," he cut her off, flicking off the light and plunging the hallway into darkness.

Tristan didn't wait for Ariel to respond. He assumed she'd do what he'd asked her to. For the baby's sake as much as her own.

He jogged back into the office, called for Jesse to heel and then made his way to the front door. Someone was outside. That much was certain. Jesse knew the difference between a person walking past and someone lurking nearby. He only barked when he sensed danger.

He was barking loudly, doing everything he could to get his message across.

"Cease," Tristan commanded, and Jesse went silent.

The office window looked out into the backyard. They'd go out the front, move around the side of the building, and hopefully surprise whoever had been trying to peek inside.

The sun had set, hints of light still flecking the horizon and turning the evening a dusky blue. There were few houses on Ariel's street, the dead-end road isolated. Maybe she'd intended it that way, but it wasn't the best situation for a woman alone. A *pregnant* woman alone. She might be fit and tough, but the baby would slow her down if she ran into trouble.

He surveyed the front yard, eyeing the house across the street. The lights were on there, a Toyota Camry parked in the driveway. To the left, a small rancher stood about a half-acre away. To the right, an empty lot stretched toward a fenced property. Plenty of places for someone to stay hidden. Watching a house like Ariel's was as easy as taking out binoculars and looking through them. She had no large trees. No shrubs. Nothing to block a person's view of the front door.

That worried him.

Someone had been outside.

He was certain of that. Jesse never issued a false alert.

The gunman? If so, the guy was taking his sweet time acting. He could have fired a few shots in the window in the hope of hitting his target. That's what he'd done at the school, firing blindly as Ariel disappeared around a corner, and then again while she was on the other side of the door.

Why wait this time?

The question made him cautious. He didn't pull his gun, just let Jesse have his lead, following the dog around the corner of the house. Tristan stopped there, listening to the night sounds—a few birds calling in the distance, an animal rustling in the bushes a few feet away.

Not a sound from the backyard. No footsteps. No sign that the perpetrator was attempting to enter the house, no indication that he was leaving. But someone *was* there. Jesse clawed at the ground, twitching in his desire to finish what they'd started.

Tristan held him back, creeping closer to the edge of the house and peering around the corner. He could see someone, a dark shadow backlit by the porch light, pressing against the screened window.

A man?

If so, he wasn't a tall one.

"Police!" Tristan warned. "Don't move."

The person jumped, nearly falling over in his haste to move away from the window.

"One more step, and I'll release my dog," Tristan warned.

The person either didn't hear or didn't care. He took off, running down the porch stairs, flying across the yard, a hood pulled up over his hair and shrouding what looked like a pale face.

Caucasian. Five-six. Slight build.

He filed the information way as he released Jesse's lead.

"Get him!" he commanded, and the dog took off, closing in on the perpetrator in the blink of an eye.

FOUR

A woman screamed, the sound chilling Ariel's blood. She wanted to run outside, see what was going on, try to help if she could, but Tristan had been right—she had more than herself to think about.

She pressed against the hallway wall, her heart thundering in her chest, her stomach in knots. Everything had been fine that morning. Sure, she'd had the eerie feeling she was being watched as she'd left for school. Sure, she'd thought she heard someone walking through the hallway behind her as she'd made her way to her classroom, but she'd always had a big imagination, and she'd chalked it up to that.

No way could anyone have followed her from Las Vegas. Even if someone could have, why would they? She had no enemies. The only person she'd given the police information about was dead.

She should be safe and happy and preparing for her daughter's birth. She wasn't any of those things, and if she was honest with herself, she had to admit that she hadn't been in months.

The house fell silent, whoever was outside was quiet. Jesse wasn't barking. The woman wasn't screaming. Tristan was obviously handling whatever he'd found.

Whoever he'd found?

Had there really been someone outside the window? Jesse had sure been acting as if there was.

The faint sound of voices drifted into the house. A man's. A woman's. Or, maybe, a girl's. No gunshots. No more screams. Whatever danger had been there seemed to be gone. She turned on the light, the crystal prisms on the chandelier sending rainbows across the gleaming floor. Tristan had closed the door when he'd walked outside.

She could open the door, go outside and see what was going on.

Or…she could stay where she was and hope that Tristan returned eventually.

She'd never been one to wait around for others to do what she could. She walked to the front door and had her hand on the knob when someone knocked.

She jumped back, biting back a scream.

"Ariel?" Tristan called through the thick wood, and she opened the door.

Tristan looked furious.

That was her first thought.

Her second thought was that he had good reason to be.

His sister, Mia, stood beside him, her face set in the perpetual scowl that Ariel had been seeing every day for weeks.

"Mia!" she said, surprised that the teenage girl was on her front porch. "What are you doing here?"

"That's exactly what I was trying to find out," Tristan muttered, giving his sister a gentle nudge into the house.

"I…" Mia began, and then shook her head, her straight dark bangs falling across her eyes.

"Spill it," Tristan demanded, and Mia scowled.

"How about we discuss it over some lemonade or ice tea?" Ariel suggested. There was no sense standing in the foyer staring each other down, and it was obvious Mia had no intention of speaking. Not yet.

"I don't believe in rewarding poor behavior," Tristan replied. "She was outside looking in your back window. That doesn't earn her a glass of lemonade."

"What does it earn me? More time alone at the house?" Mia retorted.

"No phone," he growled. "No TV. No visits with Jenny, either."

That seemed to get Mia's attention.

The teen scowled and crossed her arms over her stomach. "That's not fair. I only came here because I heard someone had been shot at the high school. I knew you and Ms. Martin were supposed to be meeting there."

"You went to the school?" Tristan's jaw tightened. "I told you to go straight home after school and get some of the work that you're missing done."

"I did go straight home."

"And then you went to the school?"

"No, I went to Jenny's house. She lives right behind Ms. Martin's place."

"Jenny Gilmore?" Ariel knew that the two girls were best friends, but she'd had no idea that Jenny lived on the property behind hers. She'd been too busy trying to get ready for the baby to do much more than introduce herself to the neighbors who lived on her street. No way would she have walked the mile and a half through scrub and trees to knock on the farmhouse door.

"Yes. She lives with her grandmother."

"I did know that. I just had no idea they were so close. I would have gone and visited before now."

"Her grandmother doesn't like visitors," Mia said quickly. "She doesn't hear all that well, and she's really ancient. She gets tired out."

"And, yet, you decided it would be a great idea to spend the evening with her?"

"She gave me a ride, Tristan. And she was going to drive me home."

"Do you really think I want you riding around with someone who is *ancient and tired out*?" Tristan's blood was obviously boiling. It was just as obvious that he was trying to keep his temper under control. "Mia, I have talked to you about this dozens of times. You can't leave the house without letting me know where you're going."

"I called you at work. You weren't there."

"You knew I wasn't there."

"No, I—"

"Tea or lemonade?" Ariel cut in. She figured that if she didn't, the two would be arguing all night.

"Neither," Tristan responded. "But thanks. We're going to get out of here. I'll be by tomorrow morning to put in the door. If you have any trouble before then, don't hesitate to call 911." He pulled a business card out of his pocket, scribbled something on the back and handed it to her. "That's my personal cell phone number. I think the one you have on file at the school is my work number. If you even have a feeling that something isn't right, I want you to call me. Don't worry about being wrong or bothering me for nothing. I want to be bothered, and I want to check out anything that seems even a little bit suspicious."

"I appreciate that, Tristan."

"Don't just appreciate it. Act on it. You can't take chances, Ariel. You've got two lives depending on you."

He took his sister's arm, tugging her back outside.

Ariel stood in the doorway as they walked to his SUV, his words echoing in her head. She hadn't needed the reminder that it wasn't only her life on the line. Every minute of every day, she felt the heaviness of the baby, the life wiggling and kicking and growing inside of her, and she felt the weight of her responsibility to her daughter.

Tristan opened the back hatch of the SUV, and Jesse jumped in. Then, he turned to face the house, his expression hidden by the darkness.

"You'd better head inside," he called, and something in her warmed at his words, at the fact that he hadn't been so focused on his sister's trouble that he'd stopped worrying about her.

"I will."

"Now would probably be best. Lock the doors and pull the shades, and stay away from all the windows. Okay?"

"You don't think the guy from the school is going to come here, do you?"

"I think it's always better to be safe than to be sorry. I'm going to ask Chief Jones to send a patrol down your road a few times a night until we figure out who was at the school."

"Thanks."

He nodded. "Mia and I will be here early. I can install an alarm system if you want. That might make you feel more secure."

Nothing was going to make her feel more secure.

Not until she knew exactly what was going on.

She closed the door anyway, sliding the bolt home, and that little bit of warmth she'd felt when Tristan was there seeped away.

She should have felt safe in her little house on her quiet road. She should have felt as though everything that had happened at the school was just a fluke, some weird anomaly that wouldn't be repeated. She couldn't help thinking about Mitch, though, about the trouble he'd gotten himself into before he'd died.

He'd been in deep with people who'd had a lot to lose

if his crimes were discovered. The Las Vegas police had assured Ariel that none of those people would care about coming after her. She had no information about Mitch's contacts, no knowledge of anything besides the basics— trips he'd taken for *work*, dates and times that he'd left and returned. She'd always kept a calendar, and she'd had every one of his trips jotted into it.

The police had used that to tie Mitch in with arsons that had occurred at businesses all over the country.

Insurance fraud.

No one had been hurt except the companies that had to pay out millions of dollars.

Typical of Mitch, he'd probably thought that made it okay.

Just like cheating on her because she was boring was okay.

She winced at the memory. The look on his face when she'd confronted him, the complete lack of remorse had shocked her.

Or, maybe it hadn't.

She'd realized long before then that he wasn't the man she'd thought she'd married.

She turned off the downstairs lights. She probably needed to eat, but she wasn't hungry. She was just tired. For the first time in a long time, she wished things could be different, that she had someone in her life who could stand beside her, offer her support, give her all the things she'd thought that Mitch would.

Tristan had done that to her.

He'd reminded her of what it felt like to have some-one care. Sure, he was just doing his job, but she'd still felt safe when he was nearby. She'd needed that. Maybe she still did.

"It's just us, though, sweetie," she said, patting her

belly as she walked up the stairs. "And, that's going to be just fine."

The baby kicked as if she agreed.

That was something to smile about.

No matter what happened, they really would be just fine.

Ariel had to believe that. She had to trust in it. God had a way of making things okay. She just had to keep moving forward, keep praying, keep hoping.

Everything else would come together in its own sweet time.

Tristan didn't say a word to Mia as he drove home.

He was afraid of what he might say and of how it would sound. He was angrier than he'd been in a long time. His sister had a right to be confused and maybe a little unsure. They'd moved from the only home she'd ever known so that he could attend the program at Canyon County K-9 Training Center.

She didn't have the right to wander around town without permission. Especially not when there was a murderer on the loose.

He'd told her that. Repeatedly.

Yet, she'd still gone to Jenny's without permission, left there to go to Ariel's house. Also without permission.

Ariel...

He'd hated leaving her alone at the house.

He needed to call Chief Jones and make sure that an officer would patrol her street for the next few nights. It wouldn't take Tristan long to secure her house. It might take less time for the perpetrator to return to finish what he'd started in the school.

His hand tightened on the steering wheel, his muscles tense at the thought of Ariel being attacked again.

"You're mad," Mia accused, finally breaking the silence.

"Shouldn't I be?"

"No, because it's all your fault I keep getting into trouble. You forced me to move here."

A lie, and she knew it. They'd both agreed it would be a good move. "That's not true."

"It feels like it is," she responded sullenly.

He pulled into their driveway, then grabbed Mia's hand before she could get out of the car and run inside. "We're not finished our conversation."

"We never have conversations. You just sit and tell me what you think I should do."

"Is that how you see things?" he asked, because he tried to be open with her. He tried to listen to what she had to say.

She sighed. "No. Not really."

"Then, what's going on?"

"I keep telling you nothing is going on."

"You were a straight-A student in Phoenix, Mia. The work here isn't any tougher."

She dropped her gaze, fiddling with one of the dozen bracelets she had on her wrist.

"Mia?" he prodded, and she shrugged.

"I told you I was going to do better, and I will."

"Ms. Martin said you have an assignment due on Monday."

"I'll do it."

"And extra credit assignments due by Friday."

"I'll do those, too."

"While you're working so hard on those, who's going to take care of Sprinkles?" he asked, pointing to the puppy that was standing in the living room window, barking frantically for them to come in the house.

"I'll take care of her, too."

"Mia, a puppy deserves more than what you're giving her," he said gently, because he didn't want to make accusations, and because he knew teenagers were notoriously bad at taking responsibility. Still, he'd only gotten the puppy because his coworker Ellen Foxcroft had suggested it might be good for Mia.

Mia looked at the puppy, and her face fell. The next thing he knew, tears were streaming down her face.

She jumped out of the car, ran to the house and was inside before he opened the hatch and let Jesse out.

He followed her inside and found her in her bedroom, the little brown-and-white mutt they'd adopted from the shelter in her lap. The puppy was licking the tears off her face.

She didn't look at Tristan as he crossed the threshold, checked the lock on her window and pulled down the shades.

He wanted to say something that would bridge the gap between them, he wanted to tell her that he understood how it felt to be a teenager, that he knew how easy it was to get distracted by friends and movies and books.

He didn't think she'd hear what he was trying to say, though.

Lately, all they did was butt heads.

It had to be something that he was doing wrong, but no matter how hard he tried, he couldn't seem to make it right.

He walked back into the hall without saying a word, and was surprised when Mia called out to him. "I'll do better, Tristan. I told you I would, and I will."

He walked back to the doorway, stood in the threshold. "I know you want to do better, but improvement takes a lot of hard work and focus."

"I am focused. Jenny and I were working on our papers together. That's why I went to her house." She kissed Sprinkles's fluffy head, scratched the puppy's belly.

"It's not about you going to her house, Mia. I think you know that."

"I did call your office," she said, and she was finally looking straight at him. He could see the young woman she was becoming. Not the little girl she'd been. Not the shy preteen he'd moved in with after their parents died. In a few years, she'd be an adult, independent and ready to face the world.

He had to prepare her for that.

And, it terrified him more than just about anything else he'd ever had to do.

"You should have called my cell phone."

"I know."

"Then why didn't you?"

"Because I thought you'd say no."

"I would have."

She nodded. They were at a stalemate. Just like always.

"Jenny is a nice girl, Tristan. She doesn't do the kind of stupid things other girls our age do," Mia said.

"What stupid stuff?"

"Chasing boys. Wearing clothes that are too mature. Swearing. Drinking."

"Who's drinking?" he asked, and she sighed.

"You're missing the point. Just like you always do." The barb hurt, but he kept his mouth shut and let her finish. "Jenny doesn't get into trouble. She likes animals. Just like me. She loves dogs. We have a lot in common."

"Including failing ninth grade."

She flushed. "That was stupid of both of us. I told her that today. I told her that we have to get serious if we're going to graduate and go to college."

"And she said what?"

"She agreed. That's why we were working on our English assignments together."

He wanted to believe her. He really did, but he'd heard the same thing a dozen times before, and he'd seen no improvements in Mia's grades or her behavior. "Tomorrow, we're going to Ms. Martin's house. She's going to tutor you while I—"

"Are you kidding me?" she nearly shouted.

"No."

"I can't have my teacher tutor me. Every kid in town will find out and be talking about it."

"You should have thought of that before you decided to fail summer school. We need to be there early. I've got a meeting in the afternoon that I can't miss. Set your alarm for seven."

She frowned, but didn't say another word.

Which was better than usual, so he'd just have to be thankful for it and move on. "Dinner will be ready in a half hour."

"I ate at Jenny's."

Another thing they'd talked about. Jenny's grandmother was on a fixed income. She couldn't afford to feed another teenager every night. Even if she could, she shouldn't have to.

He let it drop.

He'd been letting a lot of things drop lately. For the sake of harmony. Which they never seemed to have anymore.

If his mother had been around, she could have given him some advice. Of course, if she'd been around, she'd be raising Mia, and he'd still be in the army. He'd loved the military, but it wasn't the life he'd wanted for his sister— traveling from place to place, making new friends every couple of years. She'd needed stability, and he'd wanted to offer her that.

The gig in Desert Valley was supposed to be short-term.

That's what he'd told Mia when he'd talked to her about it the previous year. He'd been certain he could get assigned to the K-9 unit in Phoenix. He'd grown up there, had attended school there, and because of that, he had friends and connections in the area. His parents had lived in the same house for thirty years, and their neighbor was the chief of the police department. When he'd heard about Tristan's plan, he'd promised him a position on the Phoenix K-9 unit.

That had seemed too perfect to pass up, and Tristan had offered his parents' house as a short-term rental to friends from church, moved Mia to Desert Valley and begun the program at the Canyon County K-9 Training Center. He'd assured his sister that they'd be heading back to Phoenix in a few months, that she'd be back with her old friends and in her old school.

Things hadn't turned out that way. Until the murders, suspicious deaths and attacks were solved, all five K-9 rookie graduates of the training center were assigned to the Desert Valley PD. Mia wasn't happy about it. Tristan couldn't blame her, but he was tired of the acting out, the poor grades, the bad attitude.

His coworker Whitney Godwin had assured him that Mia's behavior was normal for girls her age. Maybe, but Mia had always been like their mother. Kind, easygoing, quick to lend a hand. She loved her friends, loved animals, dreamed of being a veterinarian or a dog trainer.

She could be either of those things or both of those things. She was extremely bright and she used to be really driven.

That had changed in the past few months.

Tristan was praying it would change back. He didn't know how much more conflict either of them could handle. He had nightmares about Mia running away and taking to the streets.

"Don't borrow trouble," he muttered, walking into the kitchen and opening the refrigerator.

"Did you say something, Tris?" Mia called from her room, and she sounded just like she use to. Happy and well-adjusted. A teen who'd been through the death of her parents but who'd be just fine.

"Nothing important." He eyed the contents of the fridge. They were pitiful. A few slices of cheese, a third of a carton of milk, a couple of grapes and an apple. Which was odd, because there'd been a dozen eggs, a head of lettuce and a bunch of fruits and vegetables earlier in the day.

"We need to go to the grocery store," Mia said from behind him, her voice soft and just a little apologetic. "I kind of brought some things over to Jenny's when I went."

He turned to face her, his heart catching just a little when he looked into her eyes. They were almond-shaped like their mother's, the high arch of her brows exactly the same as their father's.

"You brought a lot of things over to Jenny's," he said, and she sighed.

"I got carried away. The thing is, they don't have much. Sometimes they've got a can of tuna and a box of toaster pastries. Jenny is always hungry, and we always have plenty." She shrugged. "I'm sorry, Tristan. I know I messed up again. Sometimes, I forget to use the brain God gave me."

"You were using your heart. That's just as important."

She smiled at that. Probably the first smile he'd seen

in a month. "Thanks. If you want, we can go to the store now. We're almost out of puppy chow, and we can get some while we're there."

"We're out of puppy chow?" He opened the pantry where they kept it and saw the twenty-five-pound bag lying on the floor empty.

If there was three pieces of kibble in it, he'd be surprised. "I bought this four days ago," he said as much to himself as to Mia.

"Sprinkles is still growing. He needs a lot of food." Mia still sounded pleasant enough, but she'd balled her fists and looked ready for another fight.

She just might get it.

His day had started before dawn, and he'd been running ever since. He was tired, and he didn't want to deal with another crisis. Which this was about to become, because there was no way the fifteen-pound puppy could have eaten that much food that quickly.

"Mia," he said, lifting the empty bag, "What happened to the dog food?"

"I told you, Sprinkles ate it." Her cheeks were flaming red, and he knew she was lying. She knew that he knew, and that was going to make the entire conversation more difficult.

"Your puppy weighs fifteen pounds."

"He's a big eater."

"Then he's going to be awfully hungry tonight," Tristan commented, tossing the bag into the recycle bin.

"You're not going to get him more food?"

He would. The puppy didn't deserve to be punished for whatever Mia had done. "I spent a good amount of money on the food that was in that bag. It should have lasted weeks."

She didn't say a word, just dug in her pocket and pulled

out a bunch of crumbled bills. "Here's my allowance. Use that to buy the stuff."

She tossed the money onto the counter and stormed away.

He didn't go after her. He wanted to, because he wanted to tell her that it wasn't about money. It was about trust. It was about the lies that she seemed to tell all the time lately.

He wasn't in the mood to start a war, though, so he left the cash on the counter, grabbed his keys and headed to the store.

FIVE

Late pregnancy made it difficult to sleep.

Fear made it even harder.

By five in the morning, Ariel had given up. By six, she'd showered, dressed and prepared a lesson plan for her tutoring session with Mia. The teen had a lot of work to do if she was going to pass the summer course. Tristan seemed determined to make sure she did, and Ariel hoped that Mia would go along with the plan.

She set a kettle on to boil, grabbed a tea bag from the cupboard and dropped it in a mug, resisting the urge to lift the curtains and look out into the backyard. All night long, she'd imagined someone sneaking through the empty field behind the house. She'd imagined the sound of glass shattering, imagined her own panic, her trembling fingers as she dialed 911.

She'd kept the card Tristan had given her on the table near her bed, and she'd memorized his number before she'd turned off the lights.

She'd been as prepared as she could be, her bedroom door locked, a butcher knife on her dresser, but she hadn't felt safe.

The kettle whistled, and she poured hot water over the tea bag, grabbed a couple of crackers from the cupboard and headed back upstairs. She had a small study there, a bedroom for the baby and one for herself. It was a nice-sized house on a nice-sized piece of land in a nice community.

She'd been excited to buy it and to begin her new life. When she'd gotten the job offer and moved to town, she'd told herself that she'd turned the last page of a really horrible book, and she was about to read a new one. Write a new one? It hadn't mattered to her. She was just glad to be done with the past. All the ugliness of it—the marriage that hadn't been anything like what she'd planned, the divorce, the horrible moment she'd learned the truth about Mitch.

But, yesterday? That had scared her. It had made all the things she'd ignored, all the tiny little shivers of fear, the moments when she'd felt watched and hunted, seem like more than her imagination working overtime.

Had she brought her Las Vegas troubles with her?

Was someone who'd been affiliated with Mitch coming after her? Maybe seeking revenge for something she didn't even know she'd done?

She'd called Detective Smithfield from the Las Vegas Metropolitan Police Department the previous night. He'd been in charge of the insurance fraud investigation against Mitch. He'd assured her that there was no one that would put her name together with Mitch's. She had nothing to worry about. The case was closed, the people who'd paid Mitch were in jail. No one had any reason to come after her.

But, someone had been in the school last night.

That person had nearly killed her.

A childish prank gone wrong?

That's what Chief Jones had speculated. She'd called him the previous night, too, and the conversation hadn't made her any more comfortable with the situation. They hadn't found the perpetrator. They hadn't been able to pull any prints from the doors. There were no security cameras in the school. The district was too small, money too tight for those kinds of expenses.

She frowned, settling into the chair and sipping her tea. Sunlight streamed through the window, dust motes dancing across the room. It was already warm, the unair-conditioned house still sweltering from the previous day. She planned to have central air installed at the end of August, when prices went down. Hopefully, Mia wouldn't be too miserable working in a hot house.

Who was Ariel kidding?

Of course, Mia was going to be miserable. And not because of the heat. No teenager wanted to be tutored by her teacher. Especially not a teenager who was already in summer school.

Had Tristan broken the news to her, yet?

Were the two going head-to-head over it?

Probably, and Ariel was just curious enough to want to call Tristan to see if he needed any help convincing his sister to attend the tutoring session.

She wouldn't, because it wasn't her business to get between the brother and sister.

She also wouldn't because she wanted to so much.

The fact was, she'd thought about calling Tristan a dozen times the previous night. Every creak in the house, every brush of branches against the siding, and she'd grabbed for the phone, her heart pounding frantically. She'd known there was no one in the house, but she'd almost called Tristan anyway. Anything to feel less alone.

She opened the window that looked out over the backyard, letting a balmy summer breeze into the room. The sun had already risen over the trees, the gold-and-purple sky hinting at the beautiful day ahead.

She wanted so badly to be thankful for that.

She was *going* to be thankful for it. God had provided everything she needed and most of what she wanted. So what if her marriage had fallen apart, if her dreams had been shattered? She had new dreams to pursue. God would bless that. She had to believe it, or she'd spend her nights tossing and turning and worrying about the future.

She returned to her desk and thumbed through a few assignments that still needed grading. Monday would be there before she knew it, and she'd be back in the classroom.

At least that never changed—the chalky scent of the air, the waxed floors, the morose teens who, just a few years ago, were giggling little kids.

She took a sip of tea and caught just a hint of something in the air.

Gasoline?

Surprised, she walked to the window and inhaled. There it was again. The same acrid scent.

Odd. None of her neighbors were close enough for her to smell exhaust from a car or gasoline from an old lawn mower. Even if they were, it was Saturday morning, the street quiet.

She walked into the hallway and stood at the landing at the top of the stairs. Nothing there. Whatever she was smelling was outside, and there was no way she was opening a door to figure out what it was or exactly where it was coming from.

Not after what had happened at the school.

She'd almost died. The bullet had been inches from hitting her. A little better aim by the gunman, and she'd be in a hospital or worse, and the baby...

She couldn't dwell on that.

If she did, she'd be too terrified to function.

She walked into the nursery. Nothing there. Into her room. Nothing. Finally, she returned to the study. The smell was stronger now, and it was mixed with something else.

Smoke?

Fire?

Her stomach churned, her heart skipped a beat as she ran back to the window. She expected to see something. Maybe a brush fire in the woods behind the house. Instead, black smoke billowed past the window, pouring up into the sky from somewhere right below.

The back porch?

Was it on fire?

Flashes of red and orange shot through the blackness, and she could feel heat simmering in the air.

A siren screamed, the shrill sound jolting her into action.

The fire alarm!

The house was on fire!

She ran to the bathroom and grabbed a towel, soaking it in water and wrapping it around her lower face. Smoke billowed up the stairs, filling the hall with noxious fumes. Was the fire on the porch? In the foyer? At the back of the house?

Glass shattered and black smoke poured up the stairwell, filling the upstairs hallway, seeping through the wet towel and into Ariel's nose and throat.

She coughed, gagged, her eyes streaming with tears as she dropped onto all fours, trying to get closer to the ground and away from the rising smoke and heat.

She needed to get out.

She needed to do it quickly.

If she hadn't been pregnant, she would have lowered herself out an upstairs window, dropped to the ground below and run to the neighbors to call for help.

She *was* pregnant, though, and she didn't want to risk harming the baby. She had to find another way out. *Quickly,* because the upstairs hall was dark with smoke, and she could barely see her hands on the floor.

She crawled in the direction of the stairway, the baby wiggling and kicking. Was she getting enough oxygen? Was the thick smoke hurting her?

Please, God, protect her. Please, help me find a way out.

Her hand slid over the lip of the first step, and she knew exactly how many steps it would take to get to the landing, how many stairs from there to the first floor.

One.

Two.

Three.

She counted mentally. The smoke was so thick her head swam, her lungs burned from lack of oxygen.

All she had to do was make it to the door.

She scuttled downward through the haze, moving as quickly as she could. Halfway down, she hit the landing. The smoke was thicker there, heat pulsing upward. Something thumped on the stairs below, and she thought she saw a dark shadow through the gloom.

A neighbor coming to help?

Tristan? Her heart jumped at the thought. Had he arrived with Mia, seen the fire and broken in to help her?

"Tristan?" she called, her voice muffled by the towel. "Up here!"

"Good," someone said. Not Tristan. She was sure she'd have recognized his voice. A man, though. She was certain of that.

"Did you call the fire department?" she asked, and the man laughed, a mean, hard sound that made her blood run cold.

"Why would I?" he asked.

There was a flurry of movement, a flash of light and flames shot up from the bottom step.

She scrambled back the way she'd come, running from the spreading flames and from whoever had been standing at the bottom of the stairs.

Tristan saw the smoke before he turned onto Ariel's road—black tendrils spiraling up toward the sky. Not a typical sight in Desert Valley especially not at the end of a hot summer. He eyed the growing cloud. It wasn't from a fireplace or wood burning stove. Not from yard waste being burned, either. To him, it looked more like a structure fire. He scanned the houses that lined the street, and that feeling he got when things were off, the one that told him that danger was nearby, edged along his spine.

He and Jesse had trained in arson detection, and he could smell gasoline and burning wood in balmy morning air.

"Call 911," he told his sister.

Mia didn't ask why.

She pulled out her cell phone and dialed.

"The operator wants to know what the emergency is," she said a moment later.

"House fire," he responded, his gaze on that smoke as he rounded the corner onto Ariel's street.

Plumes of smoke speared the pristine sky, staining the bright blue dusky brown black. Now, he could see where they were coming from—Ariel's place. Smoke wafted up from the back of the house, and the front door seemed to be in flames, tongues of fire licking the old wood.

He slammed on the brake, shouting the address to Mia. She repeated it to the 911 operator as he got out of his SUV.

"Stay here," he commanded, then took off running toward the old house. By the time he reached it, the front door had been consumed, flames lapping up the frame and licking at the upper story. No way to get in there.

He raced to the back of the house, hoping to gain entrance there. The back deck was engulfed, the door beyond it hidden by flames.

Odd that both entry points were on fire.

The thought flitted through his mind. He tucked it away for later. Right now, he had to focus on getting to Ariel. If she was still inside, she didn't have long to escape before the entire house went up in flames.

He scanned the back facade, seeing a broken window on the lower level. He thought it opened into the office. A few shards of glass littered the ground, glinting in the early morning sun.

Had Ariel escaped through the window?

If so, why break the glass? Why not just open it?

He reached inside the broken frame and unlocked the window. It opened easily, the room beyond hazy with smoke.

"Ariel?" he called, his voice barely seeming to carry above the crackling of the fire.

He stepped back and shouted up toward the top floor of the house. If she was in there, if she was conscious, she'd be at the window upstairs, not hanging around in the downstairs where the smoke was thickest.

A second-story window *was* open, the curtains fluttering outside. "Ariel?" he yelled again.

Seconds later, she appeared, her face smudged with soot, her eyes wide with fear. She had something in her hand. A sheet? A couple of blankets. "The stairs are on fire," she called, her voice hoarse. "This is the only way out."

"Do you have a ladder in the shed?"

"I usually borrow one from the lady across the street."

He could run over there, but he thought they were running out of time. The heat from the fire burned his face, the smoke filled his lungs and he was outside the building.

"We don't have time. Climb out and drop down. I'll catch you."

"I'm thirty-six weeks pregnant!" she protested, but she was already moving, her leg sliding over the edge of the windowsill, her hands clutching the frame.

"You'll be okay," he assured her, sirens blaring in the background, someone shouting from the front yard.

A neighbor with a ladder?

He didn't have time to check.

"I'm not worried about me," she responded. "I'm worried about the baby."

"The baby will be okay, too. I'll make sure of it." He positioned himself below the window, reaching up as she slid her other leg over the window frame. He could see flames eating at the edges of the roof, moving along the frame of the house.

They had minutes. Maybe less. But, Ariel seemed frozen in place, perched in the window frame and unable or unwilling to go any farther.

"Ariel, you're going to have to do the first part. Just hold on to the window frame, and let your legs drop. I'll be able to grab you and lower you down." He kept his voice calm, because he didn't want her to panic, but she needed to move. Quickly.

"Come on," he urged, and she finally did, shifting position so that she was facing the house, her feet against the siding. Her belly bumped against the house and he reached for her, grabbing her legs as she lowered herself farther down.

"Let go," he urged, all his training, all his work in arson investigation, telling him that if they didn't hurry, the house might collapse and take them both down with it.

An old building. Lots of wood. Plenty of accelerant. He could smell it in the air and in the smoke that wafted from the window.

"Let go!" he urged, and she finally did, dropping quickly, her weight falling against him, his hands sliding from her leg to her waist.

He had just seconds to set her on her feet, and then he was dragging her away, the house groaning and creaking as the fire ate it from the inside out.

"Thankfully you came when you did!" she said, her face stark-white, a streak of soot on one cheek. "I wasn't sure how I was going to get out without hurting the baby."

"You would have managed." He had no doubt about that. Whether she would have escaped injury was another story.

"Are okay?" he asked as they jogged around the side of the house.

She nodded, but her hand was on her stomach, the protective gesture worrying him.

"The baby?" he asked, and she offered a wane smile.

"I think she's fine. She's wiggling around like crazy. Must be all the excitement."

"Too much excitement. Let's get the medics to check you out." He gestured toward the fire truck and ambulance that were pulling up to the curb.

Ariel didn't argue. She must be as worried as he felt.

Heat from the burning house scorched the front grass

and the small shrubs that edged the property, the building going up like kindling.

Ariel had escaped just in time.

A firefighter ran toward them. "Is anyone else in the house?"

"No," Ariel said, then she frowned.

"You're certain?" the firefighter asked.

She nodded. "There was someone, but I think he's gone. I think he started the fire," she responded, her gaze shifting to the house. "I was trying to get down the stairs, and he was there. I couldn't see well through the smoke. At first I thought…"

"What?" Tristan prodded, and she shrugged, her shoulders too thin beneath her T-shirt.

"I thought it might be you. I knew that you and Mia were going to be there soon, and I thought you must have arrived and seen the fire. I called out, and the guy responded. That's when I realized he was a stranger. The next thing I knew, the entire staircase was in flames."

Tristan didn't like the sound of that.

He also didn't like the fact that he'd smelled gasoline in the air or that the front and back entrances had been blocked by flames.

He wanted to ask her questions, see what else she remembered about the guy in the house, but the paramedics were there, pressing an oxygen mask to her face, taking her blood pressure, checking her pulse.

Two police cruisers pulled up in front of the house, a dark sedan right behind them. A woman jumped out of it. Short and wiry with huge round glasses and wide blue eyes, she looked as if she'd been pulled out of bed—her hair sticking out in several different directions.

She darted toward them, pink slippers slapping against the ground.

"Ariel!" she cried as she skidded to a stop a few feet away. "Are you okay?"

"Yes," Ariel mumbled through the oxygen mask.

"Are you sure? I was heartsick when I got the call about the fire."

"Who called?" Ariel took the mask off, and Tristan could see the wound from the previous night—the edges of the cut butterflied together, blood seeping out from under the bandages.

"Edna. She saw the smoke and called 911, then she called me. She was worried that…" Her voice trailed off.

"That what?" Tristan prodded.

"That fire might have been started by bad wiring and that Ariel might want to sue me since I was the Realtor who sold her the house. I told her that was total hogwash. Ariel would never do such a thing. I also told her to check and make certain Ariel wasn't in the house. She refused. She said Ariel might have spent the night with a *friend*." She eyed Tristan, and Ariel's pale cheeks went bright pink.

"Tristan is actually a—"

"Officer McKeller," Tristan cut in. "I'm with Desert Valley's K-9 Unit."

"Oh!" The woman's eyes widened, and she placed a wrinkled hand on her chest. "Edna didn't mention that."

"She couldn't have known. I escorted Ariel home last night. I'm sure you heard about the incident at the school, Ms…?"

"Janice Lesnever." She offered her hand. "I've heard some good things about the new K-9 unit. Of course, the training center is fantastic. One of the best programs in the country, the way I hear things."

"It is a great program."

"Too bad so many people affiliated with it have died," Janice continued. "That's got to be hard on its reputation."

"What people have died?" Ariel asked.

"Accidental deaths," Janice hurried to assure her. "It's nothing to worry yourself about, dear."

Accidental?

Not the lead trainer's, Veronica Earnshaw. That was for certain. Officer Ryder Hayes's wife hadn't died accidentally, either. And, Tristan had his doubts about Mike, a rookie. Another rookie K-9 handler's death had also been ruled an accident, too, but K-9 officer Whitney Godwin didn't believe it. She knew Brian Miller well and insisted that he'd have never lighted candles in his home.

"How many people have died?" Ariel asked as the EMT, placed the oxygen mask back over her nose and mouth.

"You need to get plenty of oxygen to that baby, ma'am," the young man said. "We recommend that you allow us to transport you to the hospital. It would be best to have a doctor check things out."

"I need to speak with Chief Jones," Ariel said through the mask, the words muffled. "There was someone in the house with me, Tristan. I know he set the fire."

"Arson?" Janice looked shocked, her eyes wide behind her glasses. "Why would someone set fire to my house?"

Because Ariel was living in it?

After the attack the previous night, that seemed like the obvious answer.

"I'm not sure, but I plan to find out," Tristan responded.

Whoever it was, he meant business. Going inside a burning building to be certain your victim couldn't escape? That took a lot of guts or a lot of craziness. Either way, it also took a lot of knowledge about the way fires spread, how quickly they could move.

He'd talk to the chief about it. Once the fire was out and the scene cool enough to work, he'd bring Jesse in, see what kind of evidence the lab might be able to sniff out.

For now, he'd follow the ambulance to the hospital and wait with Ariel until the chief arrived.

"Everyone okay over here?" rookie officer Ellen Fox-croft called as she strode across the yard, her golden retriever, Carly, beside her. The dog pranced restlessly, ready for the work she loved to do.

"Looks like it," the EMT responded. "But we're going to let the doctors at the hospital make certain of it."

"I'd rather not," Ariel muttered, the words barely audible.

Ellen heard. She patted Ariel's shoulder. "You'll be fine."

"Not if whoever was in the house with me has anything to do with it."

Ellen met Tristan's eyes. "What's going on?"

"Arson."

"Did you get a look at the guy?" she asked Ariel.

"Not much of one."

"Any idea how he got inside?"

"Broken window at the back of the house. I think that was the entrance point," Tristan said.

"Are you going to take Jesse around to search for accelerants?"

"We're not going to be able to get close until tomorrow. The fire is still burning pretty hot."

"I'll take Carly around the perimeter of the property. She might be able to catch a whiff of the perp. It's worth a shot anyway."

She called the dog to heel and headed around the side of the house, bypassing firefighters who were already working to contain the blaze.

It would be difficult for Carly to track the perpetrator with so many scents mixed together at the scene, but Tristan knew that she and Ellen would work until Ellen was convinced there was no possible way to track the perpetrator.

"We need to head out," the EMT said as he and a crew member helped Ariel onto a stretcher.

"Maybe it would be better to wait here," Ariel responded, her face ashen, her pallor alarming. "Whoever started the fire might be waiting at the hospital to see if I show up."

"He's not going to get anywhere near you," Tristan replied, his voice hard with anger. Ariel had been attacked twice in two days. She was terrified, shaken. That couldn't be healthy for her or the baby.

He waved to Ryder Hayes who'd just gotten out of his SUV. The most experienced member of the K-9 team, Ryder had been on the force for five years. He knew the town and the people in it better than anyone else of the rookies.

Ryder jogged over, his K-9 partner trotting along beside him.

"Ellen radioed that this was arson," he said, not wasting time or words.

"It is."

"You've called the chief?"

"I'm about to."

"I'll question the neighbors, ask if any of them saw anything. Are you sticking around or heading to the hospital?"

Tristan didn't hesitate. He didn't look at Ariel for approval, either. Whether she wanted him there or not, he was going to the hospital.

"I'm going to the hospital. I'll bring Jesse back here once the fire marshal clears the scene."

"You don't have to—" Ariel began.

"I do. There's an officer waiting to escort you into the building. I'll be there soon." He brushed the smudge of soot from her cheek, nodded for the EMT to wheel her away.

"We're going find the person who did this," Ryder muttered, his gaze on the burning shell of the old house.

Easy words to say, but it might not be as easy to follow through on them.

They'd been searching for a murderer for months. So far, they'd come up empty. They were also looking for the person who'd nearly killed Ellen Foxcroft's mother.

And then there was Marco. The team hadn't been able to find the missing German shepherd puppy that had escaped—or had been set free by lead trainer Veronica Earnshaw—the night Veronica was killed. Where was that puppy? Based on the break-ins that had occurred at homes in town that had dogs, it was clear someone wanted to find that puppy. But why? And who?

And where could Marco be? He'd been missing for a few months. He wouldn't be the tiny puppy he'd been when Marian Foxcroft had first donated him and two other pups to the K-9 Training Center. How could he be so easy to hide? Tristan and his fellow rookies were missing something.

Yeah. They were batting zero, but eventually the tide would turn.

Tristan just needed to make sure Ariel stayed alive long enough for that to happen. Not just because it was his job. Because he cared. About Ariel. About her baby.

They'd come to Desert Valley for a second chance. Tristan was going to do everything in his power to make sure that they got one.

SIX

Three hours after she'd arrived at the hospital, Ariel was cleared to leave. She'd already wiped sonogram gel off her stomach, replaced the cotton gown with her yoga pants and T-shirt, washed her face and hands and tried to fix her wrecked hair. She hadn't been wearing shoes when the fire began, but a nurse had provided socks that she'd slipped on her feet.

Now, all she needed were her discharge instructions and a ride. She also needed a place to go. That was a problem that she was still trying to work through. She wasn't brand-new to town, but she was new enough to not have the kind of friends who'd offer a room for a few months. That's what Ariel was going to need, because the house was a total loss. The fire marshal had stopped by to tell her the news. Not much left, is what he'd said. He'd asked about insurance, and he'd encouraged her to call her agent immediately.

She had, and she'd been assured that the house and everything in it were completely covered. She'd have a new home, new material items, new everything that had been lost.

In a few months that she really didn't have.

The baby would be there in weeks, and she needed a

place to bring her. A hotel room didn't seem like the kind of place a newborn should go home to.

The good news? The baby was fine. Her little heart was beating beautifully, her little arms and legs were wiggling happily. Ariel had watched her on the sonogram, listened to the rapid beat of her heart on the monitor, and she'd cried. Not big huge tears, because that wasn't her thing. Just teary-eyed relief at the fact that the person who had meant her harm hadn't been successful.

Now, Ariel was waiting for the discharge papers and for inspiration. She had no wallet, no cell phone, no money, no credit cards. No ID. She was wearing soot-stained clothes, and she had no way of getting anywhere. She also couldn't think of anyone she could call for a ride. Except for Tristan. His phone number kept floating through her head, and she kept hearing the words he'd spoken right before the EMTs had carted her away. Kept feeling his fingers sliding over her skin as he'd brushed soot from her cheek.

He'd walked into the triage room minutes after she'd arrived at the hospital, told her that there was a guard stationed outside the door, and then he'd disappeared. She hadn't seen or heard from him since.

Which should have been fine, but somehow wasn't.

She felt better when he was around. Less shaky. Less scared.

Twice, she'd nearly been killed.

Twice, she'd been saved by Tristan, and she was beginning to think he was the only one standing between her and whoever was trying to kill her.

A foolish thought.

Tristan was doing his job. Just like every other K-9 officer.

He wouldn't always be around. It was only through the grace of God that he'd been there the first two times.

Maybe she needed to leave town. Again.

Start over. Again.

Maybe she needed to come up with another job, another house, another life.

The problem was, she was about four weeks away from giving birth. No one was going to hire her before the baby was born. Getting a job after the baby was born might not be easy.

"It'll all work out," she assured herself, pacing across the hospital room, restless and uneasy.

"Knock-knock!" someone called cheerfully from the open doorway.

Ariel turned to face the speaker, smiling as she met Lauren Snyder's eyes. The pastor's wife had been kind and helpful from the first day Ariel had moved to town. She'd been the first one to show up on the doorstep after Ariel moved into her house. She'd had a bunch of kids in tow, each one of them carrying a dish of food. If Lauren hadn't been the busy mother of six children, she and Ariel would have been good friends by now. As it was, they were slowly getting to know each other over Sunday morning coffee at the church.

"Lauren! What are you doing here?" Ariel asked, surprised and pleased by Lauren's arrival. Lauren was the kind of woman who knew everyone, made friends wherever she went and who cared enough to help anyone who needed it. She'd have ideas for housing. She'd also tell Ariel what she needed to hear—that God was in control, that things would work out, that she just had to keep a steady course and trust that His plan was the best one.

"Doug and I got four calls about you. We would have been here sooner, but the big kids all had sports events, and I had to find someone to watch the littles. Doug wanted to come ahead without me, but I said you'd need a woman's motherly touch not a gnarled old pastor's words of wisdom. He's parking the car." She bustled into the room, a large duffel bag slung over her arm, a tall take-out cup in her hand. "We drove by your place before we came. I wanted to see if we could salvage any of your things."

"How bad is it?" Ariel asked even though she knew.

Lauren sighed and shook her head. "The police wouldn't let us get anywhere close, but the firefighter Doug was able to talk to said the house was a complete loss."

"That's what the fire marshal told me."

"Honey, I'm just so sorry about that, but don't worry, we'll get it all sorted out."

"We? I think you're a little busy, Lauren. The last thing you need is another project."

"What's busy have to do with anything? We've got one opportunity to live this life well. I plan to be busy until the day I keel over."

"Why are we discussing my lovely wife's untimely demise?" Doug Snyder asked as he stepped into the room, his tall broad frame nearly filling the doorway.

"I was just explaining to Ariel that we plan to help her get through this crisis."

"Of course, we do."

"Really, I don't—"

"There's no sense arguing, Ariel," Doug said. "Lauren has already come up with a plan. Trying to stop her would be as useless as trying to rein in an ocean wave."

"What plan?" Anything would be better than the nonexistent plan that Ariel had come up with.

"Did you know that the church owns a parsonage?" Lauren dropped the duffel onto the bed, then handed the cup to Ariel. "That's one of those horrible healthy smoothies all the ladies at church are always talking about. I picked it up at the organic market. Banana, strawberry and spinach. It seemed like the least offensive of the choices."

Ariel accepted the cup, but didn't take a sip. Her stomach was still churning with anxiety. "Thank you."

"Thank me if it doesn't make you gag. If it does, I'll go get you a real milkshake. I might get myself one while I'm at it." She smiled and dropped down onto the edge of the bed, her dark hair springing around her head, threads of silver woven through it. "Now, about that parsonage. The church has owned it for eons."

"Fifty years," Doug corrected. "A member of the congregation lived in it for fifty years before that. From what I've heard, she married but her husband died during WWI. She never married again, never had children and when she passed away, she left the house to the church. We were offered the opportunity to live in it when we took the pastorate, but we already had four kids and another on the way. We opted to move into something a little bigger and use the parsonage for guest speakers and visiting missionaries."

"It's empty most of the time," Lauren added. "Which is a shame. It really is a pretty little house. It needs some work, but it's very livable. Doug already called the deacons, and they agreed that it would be the perfect place for you to stay while your new house is being built. Free of charge. Everyone agreed to that. A woman in your position shouldn't have to pay rent to stay in the church property."

"I really appreciate you thinking of me, but I couldn't take advantage of the church's generosity." She'd like to, though, because having a place was a lot nicer than having to find one. Especially at this late stage of the pregnancy.

"How is it taking advantage?" Doug asked. "You've been working in the church nursery for a couple of months, you help with the AWANA program. You're a hardworking young woman who has come on some hard times, and I think that the church would be lacking in compassion if it didn't step in and help you out during this challenging time."

"It's right near the school," Lauren added. "Less than two blocks away. You've probably seen it on your way to work. It's an old bungalow with a bright blue door?"

She might have seen it, but she hadn't noticed. She'd been too focused on other things. Lesson plans, plans for the baby, moving on with her life.

"That *would* be really convenient."

Lauren smiled. "For me, too. Our place is around the corner, and after you have the baby, I'll want to come visit all the time. Now that Naomi is six, I'm missing the sweet baby and toddler years." Her youngest was a wild-child, climbing and jumping and squealing during Sunday school every day. She had her mother's zeal for life, that was for certain.

"If I moved in there, I'd want to pay rent. Otherwise, it wouldn't feel right."

"We'll discuss that with the deacons and the business committee. I'm sure that we can write up some paperwork that will make everything legal and nice. For now," Doug said, "let's just get you moved in for a few days. You can see how it works for you, decide if it's something you'd be willing to do for several months."

"That's sound good," Ariel agreed. She didn't have any other options, and she was relieved to have this one. Once she got to the house, she could lock herself in and really think about her situation. She needed a plan. One that would keep her safe until the baby was born.

"Fantastic!" Lauren gushed. "Are you ready to go now? We can give you a ride, walk through it together and see if there's anything you'll need for the night. We've got a few ladies making meals and stocking the fridge—"

"Honey," Doug interrupted. "I told you to wait until Ariel agreed to the plan."

"I know, but I knew she'd agree. She's like me. Practical." She grinned. "We'll be fabulous friends one day. I just feel it. I'll bake cookies for you and your daughter, and you'll help my kids with their English papers."

It sounded nice. Like a little piece of the dream Ariel had once had.

"I'll help your kids with their English papers even if you don't bake cookies," Ariel said. If she was there long enough for that to happen. She'd planned to make Desert Valley her home. She'd planned to raise her daughter there, build friendships there, make a life that she could be content with there.

But, she couldn't do any of those things until the police found the person who'd tried to shoot her, the one who'd set her house on fire.

The same person?

Ariel thought so.

She was interested to hear what Tristan had learned.

If he ever returned.

"Oh, I'll be baking cookies," Lauren exclaimed. "My kids go through dozens a day. Speaking of kids, Rachel had a few things she thought you could wear. I bought them last Christmas, and she thought they were too fuddy-duddy for a fifteen-year-old. She packed them in the duffel. Simon grabbed toiletries from our supply room. I have no idea what he tossed in here." She lifted the duffel. "I'm hoping soap, shampoo, toothpaste and toothbrush, but it could very well be chips and soda. Fourteen-year-old boys have different ideas about necessities than adults."

Ariel laughed, some of her anxiety fading. She was still scared, still worried, but Lauren's good humor was contagious. "I have to wait for my discharge papers. Then I can leave."

"No problem. While we're waiting, we can make a list of things you're going to need right away. Is there paper around here? A pen?"

"I'll go find something," Doug offered, stepping out into the hall, and then back in.

"Never mind. Looks like the police are back. How about we go get a coffee while they talk to Ariel," he said, taking his wife's arm as Tristan stepped into the room.

He met Ariel's eyes and smiled an easy charming smile that made butterflies dance in her stomach. "I hear you're ready to go home."

"You hear right," she responded, her voice a little hoarse, her mouth a little dry.

From the fire.

At least, that's what she tried to tell herself.

She didn't believe it. Not when she was looking in Tristan's eyes, her heart galloping with something that felt a lot like joy.

"I got back just in time then." His gaze shifted to the Snyders. "Pastor. Lauren. It's nice to see you both," he said. "I'd have been up here when you arrived, but I was waiting for a coworker to pick my sister up."

"Mia was here?" Ariel hadn't realized that, but she probably should have.

"She wanted to come in to talk to you, but I told her to wait until you were a little more settled. She wasn't all that happy about sitting around in the hospital waiting room, so Ellen Foxcroft picked her up and took her to the station. She's going to do some schoolwork there while she waits for me."

"The paper that's due in a couple of days, I hope," Ariel said. It was a lot easier to worry about than everything else.

"That and a couple of extra credit projects. Ellen said she'll make her sit next to Carrie Dunleavy until she finishes."

"Carrie?" Ariel knew a few of the Desert Valley police officers, but she didn't know any of them very well. She couldn't remember Carrie.

"She's the shy, sweet young lady who works as the police department secretary, isn't she?" Lauren asked.

"Right. Hopefully, she'll be able to keep Mia on task. Although, if my sister had been a little more patient, she could have peeked in to say hello. Looks like they've unhooked you from all the machines."

"They unhooked the monitor twenty minutes ago. I'm just waiting for the nurse to come back, and then I can leave."

"You have a place to stay?" he asked.

"We're moving Ariel into the parsonage until her home is rebuilt," Lauren cut in cheerfully.

"That little house on Perry Drive?" Tristan asked, pulling out his phone and typing something into it.

"That's the one," Lauren agreed.

"I just sent a message to Chief Jones to let him know. I'd like to come over and check it out, see how secure the place is."

"That's a good idea," Doug agreed. "If you want to wait with Ariel and give her a ride, Lauren and I can go over and unlock the place, air it out a little. I don't think it's been used since last Christmas."

"Sounds good," Tristan agreed.

No one bothered asking Ariel what she thought. One minute, they were all in the room. The next, it was just Ariel and Tristan. Alone together.

"There's no need to be nervous," Tristan said, his voice soft and soothing. As if he were afraid she was going to run screaming from the room.

She wasn't, but she probably should. Run. Not scream. Tristan was trouble.

The kind that could break her heart if she let it.

"I'm not nervous." She paced across the room, fiddled with the strap of the monitor they'd used to track the baby's heart rate.

"No?" Tristan stepped up behind her, touched her shoulder, his fingers warm through her T-shirt. "Then why are your muscles so tense?"

"Someone tried to kill me. That would make anyone nervous."

It would make anyone nervous, but Tristan didn't think that was all that was bothering Ariel. He urged her around so that they were face-to-face, looked into her dark gray eyes.

"I make you nervous, too," he said, and she shrugged.

"You're different, Tristan. I'm not sure what to make of that."

"Different than who?"

She cocked her head to the side, studied him for a moment. "I'd say Mitch, but that would seem like an insult."

"Not really. Your ex sounds like a loser. I prefer to not be anything like that."

"I meant, it would seem like an insult to compare the two of you." She tucked a strand of hair behind her ear, the dimple in her cheek showing for just a second as she offered a quick smile. "Let's talk about something else."

"Like?"

"Did you find the arsonist?"

"No, but we've got teams out looking."

"So, I'm still not safe."

"No." He wasn't going to lie. "But the chief is already rolling patrol cars past the house on Perry."

"I can't believe the Snyders are offering it to me. I was so worried about where I was going to stay, and then they showed up." She grabbed a duffel from the bed, and would have probably hefted it onto her shoulder but he took it from her hands.

"And now you have one less thing to stress about." Although, she might be a little disappointed when she got a look at the place. The house on Perry was about twenty years older than the farmhouse Ariel had been restoring. Tristan passed the place every day when he dropped Mia off at school. He'd been on the volunteer list to mow the half-acre yard in the spring, so he knew exactly what kind of shape it was in. A Cape Cod style house built in the early part of the twentieth century, it had dormer windows on the upper story, a bright blue door and questionable front porch. That really needed to be fixed if Ariel was going to live there.

"I'm really thankful for that."

"Just so you know," he said, "the parsonage might need a little more work than Lauren and Doug are anticipating."

"I don't mind work."

"You're a little bit pregnant," he pointed out, taking the duffel.

"That hasn't stopped me yet."

"At some point, you're going to have to slow down."

"I'll slow down when the baby is here. Until then, I've got to keep working." She brushed a lock of hair from her cheek, her hand shaking just enough for Tristan to notice.

"You sure you're doing okay?" he asked, wishing he had the right to tell her to sit down and rest for a while.

"I'm not even sure what okay is anymore," she responded, her eyes deeply shadowed, her face pale. She'd washed the soot from her skin, but Tristan could still smell the smoke on her clothes and in her hair.

"I'm sorry this is happening to you, Ariel."

"Yeah. Me, too. I thought when I left Las Vegas that everything would be better, that all the hard times would be over. I guess I was wrong."

"By hard times, you mean what happened with your husband?" He'd spoken with a detective in Las Vegas the previous night. Jason Smithfield had been happy to tell him what he could about Ariel's ex, but he hadn't been able to add much to what Tristan already knew.

"Ex-husband." She paced back to the open doorway. "I called the Las Vegas police last night and talked to the detective who worked my ex-husband's case."

"I spoke with him, too."

"Did you?" She turned to face him. "Detective Smithfield keeps assuring me that my problems have nothing to do with Mitch."

"He told me the same. I'm curious to know what you think. *Are* your new problems related to your old ones?"

"There haven't been new and old. At least, not that I'm aware of. Things have been off since before Mitch died. He filed for divorce right before I found out I was pregnant, and during those last few weeks that we were together, I felt uneasy."

"About?"

"Everything. I'd come home from work, and I'd feel like someone was in the house even though I knew it was empty. The phone would ring, and I'd pick up, but the caller would hang up. I started wondering if Mitch…"

"Was having an affair?"

"It's so cliché, isn't it?" she said with a sad smile. "The naive wife, thinking that everything is okay while her husband cheats behind her back."

"I'm sorry." He was, because he knew the betrayal had hurt. Still, after hearing the list of crimes her husband would have been charged with if he'd lived, Tristan thought Ariel was better off without the guy.

"I was, too. Now, I look back and wonder why I was so surprised by it." She shrugged as if it really didn't matter, but he knew it mattered a lot. He'd had a few friends who'd been through similar things. The hurt took a long time to heal.

"Anyway," she continued, "I was feeling…anxious, and I told him I was worried about us. That's when he broke things off. Three days after I left, he filed for divorce. I found out I was pregnant a couple of days later. He wasn't happy when I told him about the pregnancy. He wanted me to get rid of the baby."

"Nice guy," he muttered.

"Yeah. The thing is, I was never afraid of Mitch until after the divorce. That's when he seemed to go a little…"

"Crazy?"

"Maybe. He was just really determined that I not have our baby. *My* baby," she corrected. "We both signed legal documents when we divorced. I promised to ask him for nothing. No child support. No contact. He promised to not ever seek visitation or custody of the baby."

"Seems cut-and-dried." It also seemed like the loser's way out. What kind of man walked out on his wife, filed for divorce, gave up all legal right to his child? Not any kind of man Tristan wanted to know.

"It was, but I guess it wasn't enough for him. He wanted me to have an abortion, and he just wouldn't drop the subject. He'd call three, four, five times a day. Finally, I threatened to get a restraining order."

"Did that stop him?"

"He died a few days later. I wish I could say that I was sorry when I found out, but I was mostly just relieved. I'd already been looking for a job, and I had a lead on the teaching position here. Everything should have been okay, but since the divorce, I've just never felt…safe."

"Even here?" he asked. What he wanted to say was that she was safe. That he'd make sure of it.

"For a while, I did. Then, I started to feel like someone was watching me. A couple of times, I thought I heard someone turning the back doorknob at the house. Once, I thought someone was outside the window at the school when I stayed late."

"You didn't think to call the police?"

"And say what? That I thought someone was stalking me? I didn't have any proof. Just weird feelings. Besides, nothing ever happened, so I chalked it up to lack of sleep and an overactive imagination. Maybe it was. Maybe the things that have happened here have nothing to do with the past."

That was possible. Two women had been murdered in Desert Valley. Maybe the killer was ready to strike again, or maybe the past Ariel thought she'd left behind had followed her.

"I know we asked this already, but aside from your husband, was there anyone else in your life who might have wanted to harm you? Someone you might have forgotten? Maybe just a guy you went out with after your divorce? Someone you might have shown a little interest in?"

"I'm pregnant, Tristan," she said. "Do you really think I'd want to complicate my already complicated life by adding a guy to it?"

"Not every guy is a complication," he responded, because he could imagine helping her get settled in her role of mother, supporting her as she took on the responsibility of parenting her daughter. She had some tough times ahead of her, and if he let himself, he could picture what it would be like to be part of helping her get through them.

"I know, but anything extra in my life after the divorce would have been too much. I didn't date. I didn't go to parties. I didn't hang out at singles' retreats or go searching online for the perfect man."

"How about here? Anyone who's been hanging around you at school? Someone who might have asked you out?"

She hesitated.

"Who?" he asked, not even giving her a chance to deny it.

"Easton Riley."

"The football coach?" He knew the guy—big mouth, big muscles and a little too arrogant for Tristan's liking. It didn't surprise him that Easton had gone after Ariel. What surprised him was how annoyed he felt about it.

"He asked me to dinner a couple of times, but I've been too busy to take him up on the offer."

Good, he almost said.

"Did he seem upset when you refused the invitations?" he asked instead.

"Are you kidding? The guy goes out with a different woman every few days. The only reason he asked me more than once was because he's never heard the word *no* before, and he wasn't quite sure what it meant," she retorted. She must have realized how that sounded, because her cheeks went bright red. "What I mean is—"

"You don't have to explain. Everyone in town knows the guy is a player. I'm glad you didn't have to go out with him to figure it out."

"After being married to Mitch, I can spot one a mile away," she said dryly, as she walked to the open door and glanced out into the hall. "I wish the nurse would hurry. I'm anxious to see my new digs."

She was obviously also anxious to change the subject.

That was fine with Tristan. He'd gotten what he needed.

"I'll go to the desk and ask for the paperwork. Then we can get out of here."

"That's okay. I can wait a few more minutes."

"You shouldn't have to. I'll be right back."

He walked out of the room, pulling the door shut as he left. As soon as he was out of earshot of the room, he dialed Chief Jones's number. Easton Riley had been in town for a long time. As a matter of fact, Tristan was pretty sure he'd heard that the guy had grown up there. That meant he'd been there when Ryder's wife was killed. He'd been there when Veronica was killed, too. School had still been in session, and there'd been a ball game that weekend. Tristan remembered that because Mia had wanted to attend it with a freshman guy she'd met at church.

He'd said no.

They'd had a fight.

Typical stuff, but it had been enough for the game to be seared into his brain.

Had Veronica and Easton ever dated?

Had he and Melanie Hayes had contact with one another?

They were questions worth getting answers to, leads worth following. He left a message for Chief Jones, and then went to find a nurse.

SEVEN

It took Ariel three seconds to realize that she hadn't asked Tristan one question. It took her another second to realize that he'd asked her plenty, and that she'd answered all of them. He was much better at interrogation than she was. Which was a shame, because she needed answers.

Someone had tried to kill her twice. It seemed very possible that the person would try again. Unless the police could find him and put him in jail.

Tristan had mentioned that Officer Ellen Foxcroft would take Tristan's K-9 partner, Jesse, trained in arson detection, through her house, but he hadn't said whether or not she'd found the arsonist's trail. He also hadn't mentioned what kind of evidence had been collected from the scene, whether or not any of the neighbors had seen or heard anything.

Were there any leads?

Ariel had no idea, because she hadn't asked.

But, she would, because she had a whole lot riding on the answers. She had to decide whether to stay in Desert Valley or to leave.

She frowned, walking to the window that looked out over the parking lot. Sunlight streamed from a clear blue sky and glinted off cars that were three stories below. A few people walked through the lot, some of them hand in hand, some of them huddled in groups. One or two were alone. She found herself watching the loners, wondering if they wanted someone with them or if they were glad to be by themselves.

Ariel had never wanted to be the person walking alone.

Maybe because she'd lost her parents or because she'd never had siblings. Maybe because she'd felt a little lost when her great-aunt died. Whatever the reason, she liked having people in her life. She missed her Las Vegas friends. She missed her church there. She longed for the kind of connections that lasted. The ones that were there for decades.

Even before she'd met Mitch, she'd loved the idea of going home to someone, of lying in bed knowing that she was sharing space with a person who wanted to share it with her.

She'd wanted to grow old with someone. She'd wanted to hold hands late at night, talk into the early morning hours. She'd wanted a dozen things that were out of her reach now.

That was okay.

Or, it should have been.

Lately, she'd been wondering if maybe she could have those things that she'd once longed for.

Lately?

The last two days.

And, she knew why.

Tristan.

He seemed to fill her thoughts. His warm smile, the way he always seemed to be there when she needed him, those were heady things for a woman who'd been cheated on and tossed aside.

She could switch gears and change focus. She could

be a single mother and raise her daughter without crying for all the things she didn't have, but she couldn't stop herself from wanting that deep connection with another person, that unbreakable bond that a couple should have.

She also couldn't hide from whatever seemed to be after her. That would only be putting off the inevitable.

At least, that's how it seemed to her.

She'd left Las Vegas, hoping that the anxiety and fear would stay there. It hadn't. She'd been more anxious since the move, more scared.

Now she was being terrorized by someone.

Would moving away keep her safe?

Or would she just be followed to the next town, the next job?

Footsteps tapped against the tile floor and she turned as a nurse walked into the room.

"Ready to go home?" the young woman asked.

"Yes." Even if home was temporary. At least she had somewhere to go.

"Great. Here are the discharge orders." The nurse handed Ariel a sheet of paper. "No follow-up necessary unless something changes. You'll be seeing your OB within the week, right?"

"Yes," Ariel assured her.

When the nurse left, Tristan took Ariel's arm, the duffel hanging from his other shoulder. "You want me to find a wheelchair? Usually they wheel people out of here."

"I can walk."

He glanced at her feet, raised a dark eyebrow. "In socks?"

"It's a warm day."

"Scorching might be more the word you're looking for. The sun is brutal and the pavement is hot. Your feet might burn. Even through the socks."

"After what happened this morning, that's the least of my worries."

"I know." He took her hand, pulled her to a stop. "I also know that you're trying not to think about that old house and all the things you had in it."

"Tristan—" she began, because he was right. She didn't want to think about it. She didn't want to talk about it. She just wanted to move on.

"It's tough. I'm not going to say it isn't, but you have people who care about you. We're going to make sure that you rebuild, that everything you lost is replaced." He was so sincere, his gaze so steady and reassuring that she could barely speak past the lump in her throat.

"Thanks," she managed to say.

"Thank me after we find the guy who burned your house down." He linked his arm through hers, led her into the corridor. "You game to go straight to the parsonage?"

"Where else would we go?"

"I planned to take you to your place to pick up your van, but I've got a meeting in an hour, and I need a little time to look at the parsonage. I want to check the doors and windows, see what kind of security system needs to be installed. The sooner that's done, the better."

"A security system wouldn't have helped this morning."

He paused, his dark eyes troubled. "You're right, but knowing you have one will still make me feel better."

They'd reached the elevator, and he pressed the button, urging her inside when the doors opened. He was wearing his uniform, and there was a smudge of soot on his shoulder.

She touched the spot, trying to rub the mark away.

"Don't waste your time, Ariel." He took her hand,

squeezing it gently, his fingers warm and callused against hers. "It's not coming out until I toss it in the wash."

"I can do it for you," she offered, and wished the words back immediately. Doing laundry for Tristan was not a good way to keep some distance between them.

"I'd rather you do something else," he murmured, his thumb running along the back of her knuckles, sending warmth up her arm and straight into her heart.

She pulled away, the contact making her long for things she had no business even thinking about—this man, a future with him. "What?"

"Be careful. Be aware. Don't ever doubt your gut." The doors slid open, and they stepped out into the lobby. A few people were sitting in chairs there, reading or scrolling through their phones while they waited.

"I will be. I have been. I won't," she assured him.

"Good. I don't want anything to happen to you or the baby, Ariel. From what the fire marshal said, the entire back door of your house was consumed. The kitchen was gone. He thinks the arsonist threw gasoline on the door and then lit it. Pretty rudimentary, but very effective. Especially on an old house with lots of dry wood holding it together. If you'd been sleeping, you might not have made it out alive"

"Has any evidence been recovered?" She finally managed to ask a question. Not a good one, but it was a start. Maybe her brain was starting to function again, the shock of losing her house and nearly losing her life fading away and leaving room for rational thought.

"The house is too hot. It'll be another day before we can get in there."

"How about Ellen? Did she and her partner find anything?"

"Unfortunately, no. The area was too contaminated.

Chemicals. People. Machines. Carly is a great tracker, but any dog would struggle under those circumstances."

"So, we're back where we were yesterday." She knew she sounded discouraged. She shouldn't be. She had an entire team of well-trained officers working to help her.

"Don't give up hope for a quick solution. I've got a call in to Chief Jones. I want him to do a background check on Easton."

Tristan clearly was leaving no stone unturned. "Do you really think he's behind all this?"

His tone gentled. "I don't know. But I *do* know that you're not the only woman in Desert Valley who's found herself in danger, Ariel." He tilted his head back, his frustration evident that a killer was on the loose in his town. "I have to check every possibility. Your life depends on it."

She looked at him, those blue eyes so serious. "I know that a woman was murdered a month before I arrived." The lead trainer at the K-9 center where Tristan had recently graduated. She'd also heard about the murder of another woman, a then–K-9 rookie's wife, but that had happened five years ago. "But, I don't see what that has to do with me or with Easton."

"Probably nothing, but I want to make certain there's no connection. Veronica was murdered. The wife of one of my coworkers was murdered. Marian Foxcroft was attacked in her home. It makes sense that those things might be related. If these attacks against you are, too, we need to look for the common denominator."

She nodded. She understood why he had to investigate Easton, no matter how unlikely it was that he was the killer—and trying to murder her. Then again, with everything that had happened in the past eight months, she could almost believe that a blowhard like Easton *was* a serial killer.

"Like I said, I don't know. I *won't* know until we do a little more digging." He opened the lobby door, and they walked outside.

He'd been right about the heat.

It was broiling, the sun beating down on Ariel's head as they crossed the parking lot. She could feel the pavement through her socks, searing the soles of her feet.

Maybe she should have waited for the wheelchair.

"Hot, huh?" Tristan asked as he opened the door of his SUV and helped her inside.

"I don't mind the heat. Unless it's pouring from the back of my burning house."

He smiled, reaching past her stomach and buckling the seat belt just like he had the previous day.

"I can buckle my own seat belt, Tristan," she said as he slid into the driver's seat.

"I figured you could."

"Then why did you do it for me?"

"Why wouldn't I do it for you?"

"Do you make it a habit of answering questions with questions?"

"Yes." He grinned and started the engine. "But, if you want to know the answer, I buckled it because the baby is starting to make maneuvering a little more difficult for you. I didn't think you'd want to waste time fiddling around with a seat belt when we could be heading to your new home."

He was right, and she wasn't sure how she felt about that.

In all the years she'd been married to Mitch, he'd never done something before she'd asked. He'd never lent a hand unless she'd nearly begged for help. She'd spent a lot of time telling herself it was because he viewed her as a strong, independent and capable woman. It had taken her a couple of years to realize the truth. He was so self-absorbed that he hadn't wanted to be bothered. He'd never noticed when she was sick, when she was hurt, when she was tired. If he did, he ignored it.

Had he been like that when they were dating?

She couldn't remember.

Or maybe she could, and she just didn't want to.

Mitch had been the perfect boyfriend. He'd bought the perfect gifts, said the perfect things, written the most beautiful notes, and Ariel had wanted to not be alone anymore.

"You okay?" Tristan asked as he pulled away from the hospital.

She nodded, because her throat was tight from tears she wouldn't shed. Pregnancy hormones. That's what she told herself, but she thought it might be a lot simpler than that.

The parsonage was about as safe as a chick in a hawk's nest. The window locks were ancient, the doors flimsy. If someone wanted to break into any of them, it wouldn't be a challenge to do it.

Tristan wasn't happy about that.

Ariel, on the other hand, seemed pleased, her smile genuine as she followed Lauren from one room to the other. The paint was worn, the wood floor dull, the air filled with a hint of age and must. She didn't seem to care.

"You can use all the furniture, Ariel," the pastor's wife explained as she led the way into a dining room with built-in cabinets. "Or, if you'd rather, you can buy new things, and we'll store these."

"No. This is perfect." Ariel ran her hand over the old dining room table. The top was covered with nicks and dents, but she seemed to like it.

"Let's go upstairs and look at the bedrooms. There are only two, but that will be perfect for you and the baby." Lauren grabbed Ariel's hand and hurried from the room.

Good. Tristan had a few things to say to the pastor, and he didn't want either of the women to hear.

"Pastor," he began, but Doug held up a hand.

"You don't have to say it. I know exactly what you're thinking. She's not going to be safe here."

"I want to put in a security system, new doors and windows."

"That's going to be quite an expense, but I think I can get the board's approval. With everything that's been happening lately, I'm sure they'll understand the need for extra precautions. In the meantime, maybe Ariel can get a dog. Something nice enough to be good with kids but mean enough to take a chunk out of anyone who was trying to hurt her."

"She's gone a lot. That will be hard on a dog."

"My wife and I could probably keep it for her during the day." He ran a hand over his dark hair. "The kids would love it. They've been begging us to let them have a pet, but our house is crazy enough without adding a puppy to it. This would give us an opportunity to see if we could handle it, and it would give Ariel the protection she needs."

"It's a good plan, Pastor. How about we talk to Ariel about it, see what she has to say?" Tristan liked the idea. He liked it a lot, but if Ariel didn't, the plan would be out.

"Good idea. I've got to admit, I'm worried. Not just about Ariel. I was at the hospital, yesterday, visiting Marian Foxcroft. One of the nurses said she's showing some signs of improvement."

"Ellen said that she might be responding to voices. That's a good sign. One we've all been hoping for." That was something the team planned to discuss at the meeting. If Marian woke from the coma, she might be able to tell them who had attacked her.

Might.

Brain injuries were notoriously hard to predict. If she woke, if she remembered, if she could speak, maybe Marian was the key to solving Veronica's murder. But Marian Foxcroft was much more than someone who could aid in a criminal investigation. She was the mother of Tristan's colleague. He knew Ellen was hopeful that her mother would come out of the coma. Despite the differences between mother and daughter, Ellen was counting on her mother's full recovery. Tristan was praying that she'd got what she longed for. He knew how hard it was to lose a parent, and he didn't want Ellen to have to suffer through the pain of it.

"We've been praying for Marian. Plus, everyone in town is on edge. We need answers."

"We're working hard to find them," Tristan responded. He'd said the same to a dozen people in a dozen different ways. There wasn't much more he could add. He and the rest of the K-9 team were just as on edge, just as anxious for answers as the rest of the citizens of Desert Valley.

"I know you are." Doug was silent for a moment, his gaze darting to the staircase.

"There's something else," he continued quietly.

"What?"

"Lauren asked me not to say anything, but this isn't something I feel comfortable keeping to myself. I told her that I'd give it some time, but that I'd probably talk to you."

"About?" Tristan asked, his pulse jumping a notch, because he knew without a shadow of a doubt that the next thing the pastor had to say was about Mia. She was in the youth group at church. She was in the same peer group as the Snyders' son. She'd probably said or done something she shouldn't have.

"Last week, Lauren was in Nelson's Stock and Feed. It's right outside town."

"I know it."

"Andrew Casing is the owner."

Tristan could tell Doug was taking his time for a reason. "Right."

"His daughter is in the youth group, and she's been out for a few weeks, so Lauren stopped in to see if she was okay. Turns out she just had a summer flu. Anyway, Lauren decided to pick up a bag of cat food for our neighbor. Helen is getting up there, and it's not so easy for her to get around."

That was putting it mildly. Helen Erickson had smashed through the Snyders' fence a couple of weeks ago. She'd voluntarily relinquished her license after that.

"Anyway." Doug cleared his throat, obviously uncomfortable with what he had to say. "Lauren walked into the pet food aisle, and Mia and her friend Jenny were there. Jenny had a couple of cans of dog food, and she was trying to shove them into her pants pockets. Mia didn't have anything in her pockets, not that I could see, but she did have a can in her hand. When they saw Lauren, they put everything back on the shelves and Jenny said she was playing a game, trying to see how many cans she could fit in her pocket."

"Sounds like a really stupid game," Tristan muttered.

The last thing he wanted to hear, the last thing he needed to hear, was that his sister was aiding a shoplifter.

"It's possible that is exactly what Jenny was doing and that Mia wouldn't have let her friend steal—not with a police officer for a brother. You know that, right? Kids do all kinds of strange things."

"Anything is possible, Pastor, but a lot of them aren't very probable. I'll talk to Mia."

"I hope my telling you this doesn't change how Mia feels about Lauren. Mia needs a motherly figure in her life, and we were hoping that Lauren could be that for her. Unless, of course, you find the woman God's chosen for you. Then, she'll be all Mia needs."

The woman God had chosen for him?

The thought would have been laughable a few days ago. Now? He wasn't laughing. He was thinking about Ariel. The dimple in her cheek, the softness of her hair, the way she cared about her students.

"I won't mention Lauren," he promised, pushing thoughts of Ariel to the back of his mind.

"Thanks, and I'm really sorry about this. I know it's bad timing."

"I can't think of a time that would have been better," Tristan responded, glancing at his watch. He was supposed to be at the office in ten minutes. He needed to get moving, but he wasn't comfortable leaving Ariel by herself. Not in a house like this one. Not in any house, really.

He jogged upstairs, the narrow staircase and uneven steps concerning. There was no handrail, nothing to hold on to, and nothing to grab during a fall. That was another thing that needed to be changed. He doubted Ariel could see her feet, and the height of the steps were just uneven enough to be challenging.

According to the police report, that had been the reason for Mike Riverton's death—uneven stairs, steep grade, dark stairwell, no handrail. He'd fallen, hit his head on the cement floor and died from a brain hemorrhage. It had all looked good on paper, everything lining up and making perfect sense. Except for the fact that Mike had spent most of his adult life mountain and rock climbing. He knew how to balance. He knew how to catch himself. He knew how to fall without getting hurt. Tristan had seen him in action, and he knew just how good he was. Still, if it had only been Mike who'd died under unusual circumstances, Tristan might have been able to chalk it up to a bizarre accident. The year after Mike died, though, Brian Miller was killed in a house fire.

Both had been training at the Canyon County K-9 Training Center at the time of his death. Both had died on the night of the annual Desert Valley police dance. Just as Ryder Hayes's wife did.

Coincidence? Doubtful. And Tristan didn't believe much in coincidence.

This year, though, the night of the police dance, held a couple of months ago, came and went without trouble. No rookies were harmed or died under mysterious circumstance. One, James Harrison, had even set himself up as bait. No one took it.

He followed the sound of voices into a large bedroom to the left of the staircase. It needed a good cleaning, the wood floor coated with dust, the windows grimy but Ariel was smiling as if someone had just handed her the moon.

"Isn't this great, Tristan?" She waved toward a rocking chair that sat in the corner of the room. "There's even a place to rock the baby."

"It's perfect." Mostly because it was on the second floor, and there was a lock on the door. He checked it, made sure it was working. It wouldn't keep someone out for long, but it might offer a little extra time for help to arrive.

"Does it meet with your approval?" Lauren asked.

"It will once the doors and windows downstairs are

changed." *And an alarm system is put in, and Ariel is trained in firearm safety and owns a Glock.*

"I wish there was something more we could do to make the place secure," Lauren responded, her gaze on the window and the sunlight that was streaming through it.

"Your husband suggested she get a dog."

"I don't have time for a dog," Ariel cut in, her dark blue eyes still focused on the rocking chair. Was she imagining sitting there with her baby?

"Pastor Doug said that his family could take care of it while you're at work."

"What?" Lauren squealed. "He did not say that."

"He did," Tristan responded, smiling as Lauren ran from the room.

"A dog isn't going to save me if some guy decides he wants to set this house on fire," Ariel said.

"No, but it will bark if someone gets close enough to toss an accelerant."

"I really don't have time. Dogs take training and attention and energy. I can give it attention, but I know nothing about training, and I definitely don't have the energy."

"There are older dogs at the shelter. We could find you one that is already trained, fairly low energy. Just a sweet old guy or gal who needs a home and would be happy to be your early warning system."

She frowned, smoothing the front of her shirt over her belly, her hand lingering for just a moment. "I'll have to think about it."

"Don't think too long, Ariel. Someone has come after you twice. There's no telling when he'll be back. As much as I want to be here for you every minute of every day, I can't. If I'm not here, and something happens to you, I'll live with the guilt for the rest of my life.

She frowned. "I'm not your responsibility, Tristan."

"Maybe not, but I care enough to want you safe."

Her expression softened, her eyes a pale dove gray, the rims nearly black. "I'm not even sure what to say to that."

"Just say thanks," he murmured, his hand gliding up her arm, settling on the firm muscle of her biceps.

She stilled, her eyes widening, her body leaning toward his just enough for him to know that he wasn't the only one who cared.

He could have leaned down then, touched his lips to her temple, to the hollow of her throat, to her cheek. He could have pulled her closer, tasted her lips, let himself give in to the feeling that the two of them were meant to be together. But it was too soon. For her. For him.

"Thanks," she finally whispered, stepping back, putting some space between them.

"You're welcome. Now, how about we go to the station together? I'm sure you have some questions you'd like to ask the chief. And I have a meeting. If I'm late, I'll never hear the end of it."

He offered his hand and she took it, her fingers curving through his. Her palm felt cool and soft, her grip light. When he met her eyes, she smiled. Not the easy smile he'd seen before. A tentative one that spoke of endings and of beginnings and of a dozen things he didn't think she was ready to say.

They walked out of the room like that and might have even walked down the stairs hand in hand if the stairwell hadn't been so narrow.

He wasn't sure what Ariel thought about that, but her cheeks were pink as she sidled past and hurried down the steps.

EIGHT

Tristan had never been much for meetings. He preferred action to long, drawn-out discussions. Especially discussions that reiterated earlier conversations, listed earlier facts, asked the same questions that had been asked before.

Thirty minutes after the team's meeting had begun, the chief was still doing that, reading notes from an old notepad.

A plate of cookies sat in the middle of the conference table, the goodies provided by the department secretary, Carrie, who sat in the corner with her computer, typing notes. She was a good secretary, quiet and efficient.

She also was a great baker.

Tristan snagged a cookie, mouthing "thanks" as Carrie looked up from her computer.

She blushed, her gaze dropping quickly.

As far as Tristan knew, she'd never married, didn't date and was so shy she rarely spoke to anyone but her coworkers and a few friends.

He was always kind to her, but she still clammed up when he asked her questions.

He grabbed another cookie, listening as Chief Jones listed the evidence found at the school. There hadn't been much. A few smudged fingerprints. A bullet casing. A spent shell.

"One thing we do know," the chief said, rubbing the bridge of his nose as he stared down at his scribbled notes. "The perpetrator did not use the same gun that was used to kill Veronica. It wasn't a Sig Sauer."

There was a murmur of voices from the team, all of them gathered around a conference table, most of them with their K-9 partners beneath their feet.

"Any idea what kind it was?" Ryder asked. He looked as though he hadn't slept much. Maybe his daughter had kept him awake. A single father, he worked hard to keep a balance between his home life and his work.

Tristan knew just how difficult that was and just how exhausting it could be.

"A Glock. Something anyone on the street could get his hands on easily enough."

"Which gives us just about nothing to go on," James Harrison said. His bloodhound, Hawk, raised his head from his paws, his long ears brushing the floor as he stood. James gave him a quick scratch behind the ears, but his attention was on the chief.

"Not nothing," the chief corrected. "We know what it isn't. It isn't a murder weapon."

"It could have been," Whitney Godwin replied, her blond hair falling across her cheek as she leaned forward. "Whoever fired it meant it to be. Just like he meant the fire this morning to be fatal."

"You're connecting two things that might not go together," Chief Jones said with a sigh.

That was enough to get everyone talking.

Twenty minutes later, they'd all agreed that the attacks on Ariel were related. What they couldn't decide is whether or not they were related to Veronica's death.

"The way I see it," Ellen said, brushing a few cookie crumbs from her uniform. "We've got two separate things going on. Ariel brought some sort of trouble with her. The rest? That's homegrown."

"Maybe," Tristan agreed, but right at that moment, all he could think about was keeping Ariel safe. No matter the cause of the attacks, no matter what they were connected to, he had to make sure they were stopped.

The chief changed the subject to the German shepherd puppy that had been missing since the night of Veronica Earnshaw's murder. They knew the lead trainer had been microchipping three donated puppies at the training center when she'd been interrupted by a killer. One pup escaped—or had been set free by Veronica with her last dying breath—and was last seen running down Main Street. A witness said she thought she saw a person on a bike pick up the puppy and ride off with it, but it was dark that night, the biker was wearing a hoodie and the witness couldn't even tell if it was a man or woman.

Tristan was frustrated by the lack of progress. "We have to find the missing puppy. Veronica's body was found by the open puppy gate in the yard—as though she'd dragged herself out there to let that puppy go. For a reason. And with all the break-ins in town of homes with dogs—someone is clearly looking for that puppy, too. Maybe the killer. Any more leads on that?"

"A guy just outside town insisted that he saw a kid walking a German shepherd puppy down the road," Shane Weston said, pouring himself coffee from a carafe that Carrie had brought in. "I checked it out, but there aren't any kids living near there, and no one else saw anything. I canvased the neighborhood and wrote up a report, but it's probably safe to say the lead is a dead end."

"Funny you say that," Ryder said. "I spoke to a few of

Ariel's neighbors. I was asking about the fire, and one of them mentioned that she'd heard a dog barking earlier in the morning. A puppy yipping is how she put it."

"It might have been a coyote," the chief said, jotting something at the top of the notepad. "I've heard a few of them recently."

"Even if it wasn't," Whitney added. "There are plenty of strays around. Any one of them could have a litter of babies."

"Aside from the puppy, did any of Ariel's neighbors notice anything unusual this morning?" Tristan asked.

"Not until they smelled smoke. We should be able to get into the house tomorrow. The fire marshal said the structure is sound. The house was built on a slab, so there's no danger of a floor collapse. All that's really left are four walls."

"That's such a shame," Carrie Dunleavy, the secretary, spoke quietly, her voice barely carrying across the room.

"It is, and I've got a meeting with the town council to discuss it." The chief glanced at his watch. "Seems like all I'm doing anymore is running. A guy my age needs a little bit of a break. Before I go, do we have an update on the missing evidence box?"

The question brought everyone to attention, the entire team going still and silent. Last month, someone had entered the evidence room and taken all items found at the scene of Veronica's murder. There was no doubt it was an inside job. No one but a member of the Desert Valley police force and employees of the police station had access to the room.

"I'm afraid not," Ellen said, her fingers tapping against the tabletop. "We haven't found a match for the earring found in the evidence room, either. If we find that, I feel confident we'll find the person who took the evidence."

"And maybe Veronica's murderer," Tristan said. He didn't want to think that Veronica had been killed by someone he saw every day, someone he'd spoken to, probably joked with. Trusted.

But the evidence box had been there. Now it was gone.

The only person who'd be worried about what the evidence would reveal was the person who'd killed Veronica.

"Again," the chief said with a tired sigh. "Let's not connect two things that might not be connected. Just because the evidence is missing doesn't mean the murderer took it."

"I think you're wrong," Ryder said, the blunt comment not seeming to bother the chief at all.

"You might be right, Ryder. If you are, then someone we know well is a murderer. That's not something I want to spend too much time dwelling on. I've got to go. I'll see all of you tomorrow."

The chief walked out of the room, Ryder and Whitney following behind him.

Tristan needed to leave, too. He'd left Mia and Ariel in the interrogation room just off the main corridor. Mia had taken out her laptop without being prodded, and by the time Tristan walked out of the room she and Ariel were looking at the document Mia had been working on.

That had been nearly an hour ago.

More than likely, they were both anxious to leave.

Especially Mia who'd spent most of the morning at the station hanging out with Carrie.

Speaking of which…

He turned toward the secretary, waiting as she closed down her laptop and stood.

She must have sensed his gaze. She met his eyes, offered a timid smile. "Did you need something, Tristan?"

"I just wanted to thank you for hanging out with my sister this morning."

"It was no problem. She had work to do. That kept her occupied." She tucked a lock of brown hair behind her ear, her fingernails short and unpainted. Behind her, framed photos hung from the wall, group shots of different teams that had gone through the K-9 training program. Mike was in a couple of the group shots.

He took one from the wall, eyeing his old army buddy.

Old? Mike had been in his early twenties when he'd died.

"I'm not sure the chief would want you to take that," Carrie said, and Tristan was surprised by the comment and the protest.

"Don't worry," he assured her. "I'm not taking it. I just wanted to see how Mike looked after he graduated from the program."

"Why's that?" James asked, calling for his bloodhound to heel as he crossed the room and stared down at the photo.

"It's always seemed odd to me that he died from an accidental fall. The guy was part mountain goat." Tristan scanned the photo. He recognized a few of the people in it. The chief. Ryder. Carrie. She was in the background like always, her eyes wide, her hair swept up in some kind of fancy style.

"Even mountain goats fall sometimes, Tristan," James said.

Tristan barely heard. He was too busy studying the photograph. There was something odd about it. Something he couldn't quite put his finger on.

"Is there something odd about this picture?" he asked, handing it to James.

James studied it for a couple of seconds and shrugged. "Not that I can see. Why?"

"Something about it is bothering me, and I can't figure out what."

"Maybe seeing your friend alive and healthy?" James suggested. "That's got to be hard."

"I imagine that's what it is," Carrie chimed in, her brown eyes full of compassion.

"Maybe." But Tristan didn't think that was it. He handed the photo to Carrie. "I feel like it's something else, though. You're sure there's nothing odd about it?"

Carrie stared at the photo, tilting her head left, then right. "Not that I can see." She frowned. "Mike does look tired in the picture, though. Don't you think?"

"I didn't know the guy," James said. "So I can't say for sure, but he looks pretty wide-awake and healthy to me."

Tristan agreed. Mike looked exactly like he had every time he and Tristan had gotten together. His blond hair was a little longer, but other than that, he looked healthy, strong and a little full of himself. Just like always.

"Yeah. He looks good to me, too."

Carrie nodded. "You want me to hang this back up?"

"That would be great. Thanks, and thanks for the cookies. They were fantastic."

"I'm glad you enjoyed them," she murmured, her cheeks pink, her eyeglasses falling down her nose a bit as she replaced the photo.

Tristan was tempted to look at it again, because he couldn't shake the feeling that he was missing something very important. The rest of the team had left, though, and he needed to get Mia back home. He worked the graveyard shift tonight, and tomorrow was church. He'd drop Mia off, pick Jesse up and get what he needed to fix Ariel's security problems.

It shouldn't take long to swap out a few doors and bolt a couple of windows.

He strode through the quiet corridor, the odd feeling that someone was watching him crawling along his spine.

It reminded him of what Ariel had said—the odd feeling that she wasn't alone, that someone was watching her.

He glanced over his shoulder and saw Carrie standing in the doorway, her brown eyes wide.

"Everything okay?" he asked, and she blinked.

"Carrie?" he prodded.

"Everything is great, Tristan. I was just…thinking about something. And trying to decide if I should print out the minutes of the meeting now or later."

He was tempted to tell her not to print them out at all.

No one really read them. Except for maybe the chief.

"There's no time like the present to take care of business," he said instead. Carrie had always been nice to him, had been kind to his sister this morning and he didn't want to get her in trouble with the chief.

She nodded, sliding her glasses back up on her nose. "You're right. That's exactly how I always feel. Thanks, Tristan."

She scurried away, and Tristan walked to the end of the hallway. The door to the interrogation room was open, and he could see Mia and Ariel sitting beside each other. They both looked relaxed, Mia smiling a little as Ariel said something to her.

That was a surprise. His sister didn't smile much anymore. At least, she didn't when she was around him. Ariel seemed to bring out the best in her. She probably brought out the best in all her students. She had empathy, compassion, humor. That was a great combination of things to have in a teacher. That was a great combination of things to have in a person, and Tristan couldn't deny how charming he found them.

She must have sensed his gaze. She glanced at the door, then caught his eye and smiled, the dimple in her cheek showing. "Is the meeting over?"

"For now. How's it going in here?" he asked as he stepped into the room.

"Good," Mia admitted, her normal teenage attitude gone. "We were talking about school."

"Yeah?" That was it. No questions, because he didn't want to bring back the sullen teenager he usually had to deal with. "I'm glad you were having fun. I've got some work to do over at Ariel's house. I thought I'd bring you a hamburger before I went over there."

"You've already done more than enough for me today, Tristan. Why don't you and Mia go home? You can work on the house another day."

"What house?" Mia asked, standing and stretching, her skinny body encased in her favorite jeans and T-shirt. "I thought your place burned down, Ms. Martin."

Ariel winced, but still managed to smile as she answered. "It did. I'm staying at the church parsonage until I can have a new house built."

"That little house near the school? The one with the pretty blue door?"

"That's the one," Ariel agreed.

"I heard the youth group has sleepovers there every year."

"I don't know anything about that," Ariel said. "But I can tell you that it looks like the perfect place for a bunch of kids to hang out."

"I heard there's a secret passage in the basement that goes to the church. Do you think it's true?"

"I don't know, but I'll check it out and fill you in on what I find."

"That would be awesome, Ms. Martin."

Mia sounded excited, and Ariel seemed just as excited to fill her in.

As Tristan watched his sister and Ariel talk, he wished he and Mia could share the same kind of easy back and forth. Ariel was a good influence on his sister. On him, too. He wasn't too sure how he felt about *that*, but he was going to go with it, see where it led. Where God led.

Ariel wasn't nearly as excited about the parsonage as Mia seemed to be, but she smiled and chatted about it anyway. Tristan stood a few feet away, watching the exchange. He seemed to hold back a little when it came to his sister. Maybe he was afraid he'd say the wrong thing and break the happy little conversation up. He cared about his sister. He wanted the best for her, but he had no idea how to deal with a teenage girl. Maybe Ariel could help him.

"You know what else would be awesome?" Ariel asked, keeping her voice light and her expression pleasant.

"What?"

"You passing my class so you could attend tenth grade in the fall."

"I'll pass the class if you host a sleepover." Mia laughed, the sound dying abruptly when she saw that her brother was watching.

Smile to frown in two seconds flat. Mia had perfected the art. Ariel had watched her practice it over and over again in the time she'd spent with Mia and Tristan.

There was no doubt that Tristan noticed. He didn't comment on it. Just offered his sister a smile.

"You ready to go?" he asked, and she nodded.

"I guess."

"How about you, Ariel?" he asked, and she found herself looking into his handsome face, his gorgeous dark eyes.

"What?"

"Are you ready to go? I'll give you a ride to the parsonage. The chief is going to have a patrol car parked outside today and tonight. We'll have one near the school when you return on Monday."

Was she ready to go?

No.

She felt safe at the police station, protected by Tristan and his fellow officers. She couldn't stay there forever, though. No matter how tempted she might be.

"Sure," she responded as cheerfully as she could.

Tristan didn't even crack a smile.

She was sure he knew she was terrified. He didn't feed her any false platitudes, didn't tell her that she shouldn't be scared. He just stepped aside so she could walk into the hall.

"You're not alone, Ariel," he said quietly as she moved past, the words barely carrying above the wild pounding of her heart.

She wanted to say something clever or strong, something that would let them both know that she was just fine. She had no words, though. Nothing to offer but a brief nod and a thank-you that she wasn't even sure he heard.

You're not alone.

Three words that she'd desperately needed to hear, because she had been feeling alone these past few months. Three words that reminded her that she wasn't walking the path by herself, that she had people who cared, a God who cared.

That she had Tristan.

Such a strange thought, because she'd had no intention of relying on anyone again. But maybe *reliance* wasn't the right word to describe what she felt when she was around him. Maybe *trust* was a better word. *Hope.*

She glanced at Tristan. He was watching her, his eyes shadowed with fatigue, a day's worth of stubble on his chin. He'd been working hard to find the person who was after her, and it showed.

"Thank you," she said again, and this time he heard, his expression easing into a soft smile that turned his eyes from nearly black to warm brown.

"Thank me by staying safe," he responded, pushing open the door and leading Ariel and Mia outside.

The sun was bright and hot, the sound of cars and voices drifting on the dry air. It might have been Ariel's imagination, but she was certain she could smell a hint of smoke in the air.

Or maybe it was on her clothes.

She needed to shower and change, and then she needed to get to work. Tristan had been correct about the house. As much as she appreciated what Lauren and Doug were doing, there was no way she'd feel safe until she had new windows, new doors, a security system.

A dog?

She'd always wanted a dog. Yes, she was busy, but she'd have help caring for it. She was also scared and a dog would make her feel safer.

"I wonder what time the animal shelter closes today," she said as Tristan opened the SUV's door.

"Six. I volunteer there one Saturday a month," Mia responded, getting into the backseat, and then muttering something under her breath.

"What's wrong?" Tristan asked.

"I left my backpack near Carrie's desk. I've got to run in and get it. I'll be right back."

She was off like a shot, sprinting across the pavement, her dark hair flying out behind her.

"I remember being that age," Ariel commented as Tristan started the engine and turned on the air. "It's not easy."

"I know. I'm trying to be patient with her. I'm trying to remind myself that I've never been a teenage girl, and I have no idea what she's going through," Tristan responded with a tired sigh.

"You're doing great, Tristan." She meant it. Mia might be shirking her schoolwork, she might be skipping class, but she was a nice girl who really seemed to care about her brother.

"Tell me that when she's back in ninth grade this fall."

"There are worse things than being held back a grade."

"I guess that means you don't think she's going to pass your class?" He met her eyes, and she found herself studying his dark brown irises, finding the flecks of gold and green in their depths. He had long eyelashes, dark brows and tiny lines fanning out from the corners of his eyes.

"Actually, I think she will. The first draft of her paper is really good. But, what I said still stands. There are worse things than being held back. Mia is a great young woman."

"With attitude to spare."

"She's just trying to find her way."

"If finding her way includes standing by while her friend shoplifts dog food, then she's on the wrong path."

"Shoplifting?" That surprised Ariel. She'd seen the way Mia was with the other students in summer school. She shared lunches, baked cookies, treated everyone with respect. Sure, she was different than the other girls. She had her head screwed on a little tighter, was a little more aware of how fragile life was. She didn't care about the latest fashions or the cutest boys. That certainly didn't make her a bad kid or a criminal.

"Are you sure, Tristan?" she asked, trying to see some hint of doubt in his face.

All she found was fatigue and concern.

"I'm not sure of anything except that Lauren saw them at the local feed store. Jenny was shoving cans of dog food in her pockets. Mia was with Jenny."

"Jenny I can believe. Mia…she was probably in the wrong place at the wrong time."

"I keep telling myself that's the case." He offered a tired smile, and she was tempted to touch the arm he had draped over the seat, tell him that everything was going to be okay.

"For what it's worth, I agree with you."

"Thanks."

"For?"

"Giving me hope that I'm not failing my sister and raising a criminal. I'm going to have to talk to her about Jenny. Again. That kid is a bad seed."

"Not really. She's just a young kid who's been allowed to run wild. She's got a good heart."

"Maybe, but I haven't seen much of it. Ever since she and Mia started hanging out, my sister has been a walking talking attitude."

"Jenny calls her own shots. Maybe Mia is trying to do the same. The thing is, Jenny has been with her grandmother for five years, and she hasn't had a whole lot of rules. Plus, she's smart. She can skip quite a bit of school and still do okay."

"She's in your summer school class, Ariel. Obviously, she's not doing that well."

"Last year, she struggled. She struggled for the first few weeks of summer school, but she seems to be coming around. I'd say that has something to do with your sister."

"You're trying to tell me that Mia is a good influence on Jenny so I should continue to let the two of them hang out?"

"I'm saying that Jenny is the only real friend your sister has in school. They do everything together. If you try to break them apart, you're asking for more of the attitude Mia has been giving you. If you let them continue on the way they are, you might be surprised at how things work out."

"I just want Mia to make good choices," he responded, his gaze shifting to the front door of the police station. Mia had reappeared, the backpack tossed over her shoulder. She was skinny and gangly, her arms and legs too long for her frame, her hair a little too wild around her face.

She waved as she ran toward them, and Tristan sighed.

"I'll give it a little more time, but if she fails your class—"

"She won't," she assured him as Mia slid into the SUV.

"Won't what?" she asked, her dark eyes exactly like her brother's, her lashes just as long.

"Fail my class." Ariel said. "I have faith in you and so does Tristan."

Mia raised her eyebrows. "Please tell me that you weren't talking about me the entire time I was gone."

That got almost a smile out of Tristan.

"We were also talking about Jenny," he said, the smile fading.

"Because you hate her," Mia grumbled. "And you think I'm such a wimp that I can't make my own decisions."

They were about to have an epic battle, and Ariel had no idea what to say to stop it.

Tristan's cell phone buzzed, interrupting whatever he might have said.

He grabbed it and answered quickly, his expression hard, his gaze on his sister. "McKeller here, what's up?"

There was a moment of silence, concern deepening in his features. "They're certain about that?"

His gaze shifted, settling on Ariel and staying there as he listened to the caller. "Okay. I'll let her know."

He ended the call and shoved the phone back into his pocket.

"Let me know what?" she asked, because she had absolutely no doubt that caller had been talking about her.

"The note we found at the school yesterday? The handwriting on it *does* match your ex-husband's."

The words were matter-of-fact, but she could see the sympathy in his eyes, see the concern in his face.

She wanted to tell him not to worry, that she was fine, but her throat was clogged with fear, her heart pounding frantically. There were a dozen questions she needed to ask, a bunch of things she could have said.

Instead, she turned away from his brown eyes, his sympathetic look, and stared out the window, trying to think of some explanation for the matching handwriting.

"It can't be his," she said, and she wasn't sure if she was trying to convince herself or Tristan.

He covered her hand, his palm warm against her chilled flesh. "The handwriting expert with the state police says she's 99 percent certain that it is."

"He had to have written it before he died. Do you think…?" Her voice trailed off. She didn't want to voice the thought in front of Mia. She didn't want to ask the question that was filling her mind.

Could Mitch have paid someone to kill her and the baby? Could he have arranged it all before he died?

He'd wanted them both out of his life. He'd threatened to get rid of the baby if Ariel wouldn't. Not just the first time she'd told him the news. He'd called her on numerous occasions, leaving messages in a cold tone that had left her terrified.

Get rid of the kid or I will.

She'd told herself that he hadn't meant it, but she'd never really believed that. The deadly serious tone of his voice had chilled her to the bone. If he'd been screaming, ranting, yelling, she might have been able to brush it off as emotions getting the better of him. He'd been calm, though. He'd wanted the baby gone, and he'd have probably been happy to get Ariel out of the picture, too. A clean break. Nothing to tie him to the past. He could have married the woman he'd been living with, talked her into all the things Ariel had refused.

He'd died, though, and that should have been the end of it.

Should have been, but someone wanted Ariel dead, and the only one she could think of who'd ever felt that way was Mitch.

Tristan squeezed her hand, the gesture gentle and comforting.

"I'm okay," she said as if he'd asked, and he nodded, his palm brushing against her knuckles, his hand sliding away.

"We'll talk more after I drop Mia off," he said, and she nodded, because there was nothing else she could do. They both knew she wasn't okay. They both knew that the information he'd shared changed everything and solved nothing.

Mitch had written the note.

Mitch had wanted her dead.

Everything that was happening was because of him, and she wanted to cry because of it, wanted to ask God why she couldn't just be free of the past.

You're not alone.

Tristan's words suddenly filled her head, chasing away some of the panic and the fear. She let them comfort her as he pulled out of the parking lot and headed home.

NINE

The drive to Tristan and Mia's place took minutes.

It seemed to take a lifetime.

By the time they pulled up in front of the brick rancher, Ariel's stomach was in knots, her mind filled with memories she'd been trying really hard to let go of.

Mitch at his best and at his worst. A man she'd thought she knew well who had turned out to be a complete stranger.

Someone who'd wanted her dead?

Who'd paid someone to make sure she and her child didn't live?

She shuddered.

"It's going to be okay," Tristan said as he opened his door.

"I'm glad one of us thinks so," she responded.

"It will be. Nothing can last forever. Eventually, we always get to the other side of our troubles." He glanced at his sister. "I remind myself of that every day. Come on, let's go inside. I have to get Jesse. We're working the graveyard shift tonight, and I'm hoping to take him to your house. He's trained in arson detection, and he might be able to sniff up something that everyone else has missed now that everything has settled down."

"Graveyard, again?" Mia cut in. "Are we ever just going to be a normal family with a normal schedule? The kind where the parent is actually home with his kid?"

"Eventually, but things are kind of crazy right now. You know that, Mia," Tristan responded, a hint of weariness in his voice.

Ariel had a feeling they'd had this conversation many times before and that it had accomplished absolutely nothing.

Talk was sometimes cheap. She remembered bottling up all the words she wanted to say in those final days of her marriage, shoving them down and keeping quiet, because it was the only way to keep the peace. That was something she'd coveted. Peace.

She hadn't had much of that when she was a kid. Her father had been an alcoholic, coming home at all hours of the night, tripping over things, breaking things, apologizing with slurred words and heaving sobs. By the time Ariel was nine, her mother had died of cancer, and she'd become her father's weekend caregiver, keeping the secret that her mother had kept for a decade because her father was a well-liked businessman, a deacon at church, a weekend drinker who went a little too far a little too often, but a good guy who'd loved his wife and his daughter.

He'd died while she was babysitting for a neighbor. It had been a Thursday night. Not a drinking night for him, but he must have decided he wanted to drink anyway. He'd emptied a bottle of Scotch and then gotten in the car to buy some more. He drove off the road before he reached the liquor store, flipping his car and dying instantly.

Another memory Ariel tried not to dwell on, and one of the reasons she'd married young. Her great-aunt had taken her in after her father's death, and when she'd died,

Ariel had been alone. She'd longed for someone she could connect with. She'd been desperate to have people she could call family.

Mitch had stepped into her life when she was just vulnerable enough not to notice his selfishness, his lies.

And, now, Tristan had stepped into her life.

Right when she'd decided she didn't need anyone. Right when she'd been determined to go it alone. She wasn't sure how she felt about that.

She followed Tristan and Mia to the front door of the house, only half listening to their conversation. The words seemed rehearsed, spoken so many times both had their lines memorized.

"Since you're going to be gone," Mia huffed, her backpack dragging on the ground. "I want to spend the night at Jenny's."

"Mia, I don't—"

His words were cut off by the revving of a car engine.

Ariel glanced toward the street and had just enough time to see a black car speed around the corner before Tristan yanked the door open, shoved Mia inside and nudged Ariel in after her. Mia tripped and went down hard, sliding across hard wood.

The door slammed, a burst of gunfire filling the sudden silence, Mia's screams mixing with the sound of a dog's frantic barking and a puppy's terrified howl.

"Tristan!" Mia wailed, and Ariel finally realized what he'd done—shut them in the house and shut himself out.

The first bullet missed Tristan by an inch.

The second one took a chunk out of his upper arm.

The third buried itself in the door frame.

The guy was still a bad shot.

Tristan wasn't. He'd been well trained by the army, and

he knew how to take someone out. He pulled his service revolver, aiming for the windshield of the vehicle as the car sped by.

The bullet hit its mark, shattering the glass.

The driver kept going, and Tristan fired another shot, hitting the back tire.

The sedan swerved, speeding around the block and out of sight.

Tristan jumped into his SUV, wishing he had Jesse with him. There'd been no time to get Jesse from the house, though. Not if he wanted to catch the shooter.

And, he did.

No way was this guy escaping again.

Three attempts at taking Ariel's life.

This time, the perpetrator could have hurt Mia.

Tristan never should have brought Ariel to the house. Not while his sister was there. His mistake could have cost Mia her life.

He sped around the corner, heading in the direction the crippled vehicle had gone. He could see the sedan ahead, racing toward the main thoroughfare that led to the highway.

He called in his location and asked for backup, wishing he'd had time to get Jesse. If the driver of the vehicle turned off the road and jumped out, they'd be chasing him on foot. Jesse wasn't trained in apprehension, but he could take down a man if he had to, disarm one if he saw a gun.

Behind him, a K-9 vehicle sped out of a side street, lights flashing, sirens blaring. Fellow rookie K-9 officer Shane Weston. Tristan recognized the number on the SUV, and he slowed down, let Shane take the lead. His K-9 partner, Bella, was trained in apprehension. If they could get the guy to stop, they'd have a good chance at taking him down.

Up ahead, the sedan blew through a stop sign and squealed onto the highway entrance ramp. The driver took the curve too quickly, and the sedan flew off the road, bumping down an embankment and into a ditch. The door opened, and a man tumbled out, racing away from the wrecked vehicle as Tristan stopped his SUV.

Shane was already out of his vehicle, Bella on a lead beside him, lunging toward the fleeing man.

"He has a gun," Tristan warned as he joined the two.

"And, I have Bella. Seems like he's at a disadvantage. Police!" he called. "Stop, or I'll release my dog."

The guy just kept running, sprinting toward a distant copse of trees. Maybe he thought he could find a place to hide there. If so, he knew nothing about the way K-9 apprehension teams worked. Bella already had the guy's scent. She'd follow it until she had him cornered.

"I said 'stop'!" Shane called again, then he unhooked Bella's lead and released her. The German shepherd bounded down the ravine, moving so quickly the perpetrator barely had time to respond. He'd pivoted and was turning back in their direction, when Bella hit him full force. The guy fell backward and lay still, Bella growling in his face.

Seconds later, Tristan had the guy by the wrists and was snapping cuffs into place. He patted him down, pulled out a wallet, a cell phone and a wad of twenty-dollar bills. He could feel warm blood oozing down his arm as he dragged the guy to his feet. He didn't care. He wanted answers, and the pasty-faced, pockmarked man Bella had apprehended had them.

"Keep that dog away from me," the guy howled, his mud-brown eyes focused on the shepherd.

She stood a few feet away, growling quietly, her hackles still raised.

Shane patted her back, hooking the lead back into place. "If you'd cooperated and stopped like you were told, she wouldn't have gotten close to you in the first place."

"I didn't hear you, so you had no right to sic her on me."

"You had no right to shoot at me, so I guess we're even," Tristan replied. "Or, maybe not. What you did was a felony. What my buddy did was his duty."

"I didn't shoot at you," the man spat, his eyes a little too small in his puffy face. He looked as if he'd had a few too many beers and a bit too much hard liquor. As a matter of fact, he reeked, the scent of stale alcohol wafting around him.

"Have you been drinking?" Tristan asked, opening the guy's wallet and pulling out a driver's license. Butch Harold. Forty-five. Five-foot-ten. Two-hundred-twenty pounds.

From Las Vegas, Nevada.

"Sometimes, a man needs a little liquid fortification," Butch responded, his gaze darting to Bella again.

"You're a long way from home, Butch. I guess there's a reason for that?"

"Had a job to do," Butch responded. "Now, I'm done. Let me go, and I'll just head on back the way I came."

"You tried to kill someone. You don't get a free pass on that."

"I wasn't trying to kill anyone," the guy yelled. "So, if you think that, you can just stop!"

"Tell you what," Shane said, walking over with Bella. "How about I read you your Miranda rights, and then we discuss your reasons for visiting Desert Valley?"

"I'm not here for a visit," Butch said. "And I'm not telling you squat."

Shane ignored him, reading him his rights and then escorting him up the ravine. A squad car was there, Eddie Harmon standing beside it.

"This the guy who's been trying to kill the teacher?" he asked.

"I said I wasn't trying to kill anyone. Especially not some pregnant lady."

"How did you know she was pregnant?" Tristan asked.

"The guy who paid me said, I'd know…" Butch's voice trailed off, and he scowled. "You thought you had me, didn't you?"

"I *do* have you." Tristan tugged him to Eddie's car. "You want to transport him to the station? I'll help Shane collect evidence here, and then I've got to go check on my sister and Ariel. After that, I have some questions I'd like to ask this guy."

"I want a lawyer!" Butch yelled as Eddie opened the back door of his cruiser and shoved him inside.

"We'll get you one," Eddie promised, and then he slammed the door shut.

"Good job on the apprehension. Not that he looks like that much of a challenge. He put up a fight?"

"Bella took him down. The guy took one look at her teeth and gave up," Shane responded.

"She's a good dog," Eddie said, taking off his uniform hat and wiping sweat from his temple. "But that guy is drunk as a skunk. Do you really think he's capable of going after the teacher?"

"I don't think it. I know it. He took a shot at my house. I think he was aiming for Ariel. It's hard to say, though. His aim stinks."

"Looks like it was good enough for him to take a slice out of your arm."

"He barely grazed it. I'm more irritated about the bullet slug in my door frame." Tristan took an evidence bag from his truck and dropped the wallet, phone and money into it. "These were on him. Want to take it back to the station? Show the chief the phone. He may be able to get some information off it. The rest you can lock in the evidence room."

"Who's to say the cash won't go missing after I put it there?" Eddie smirked.

"Or *before* you put it there?" Shane retorted.

"Now, wait a minute, Shane. I might joke, but I'm no crook."

Shane nodded, his attention on the sedan that was still nose-down in the ditch. "Let's check out the vehicle. Maybe good old Butch left some information that will lead us to the guy who hired him."

"If not, maybe attempted murder charges will loosen his tongue." Tristan followed Shane to the sedan and used gloved hands to open the passenger-side door. The gun was lying on the floor. A Glock. New.

"Looks like this could match the one that was used at the school." He checked the chamber, unloaded the pistol and dropped it into an evidence bag. He found a round of ammunition in the glove compartment. Registration for the vehicle. Not in the perp's name. A stolen vehicle? It seemed likely.

"I've got something back here, too." Shane lifted a paper bag from the backseat. "The liquid fortification. We can probably get some DNA evidence from it. Not that we'll need it. The guy is guilty as sin."

"We know it, but we still have to prove it in a court of law." Tristan handed him another evidence bag and popped the trunk. He expected to see something there. Maybe a few empty gas containers, matches. Something that would indicate that the guy had set fire to Ariel's house.

He found nothing. Not even a whiff of gasoline-soaked carpet.

"Strange," he muttered, lifting the carpet and opening the small hatch that contained the spare tire. It was there along with a tire iron and an electric jack.

"What?" Shane peered into the trunk, Bella's leash in his hand, the dog settled onto her haunches beside him.

"I thought I'd find something that linked him to the fire."

"Could be he got rid of the evidence. If I were him, I sure wouldn't be riding around with it in my car."

"I'd expect the gasoline fumes to soak into the interior. Leather and carpet can hold on to the scent for weeks."

Shane inhaled, shook his head. "I don't smell anything."

"I'll bring Jesse over later. If there's been gasoline in this car in the past few days, he'll know it. I need to check on Mia and Ariel first. Can you call this in? See if the chief wants a state evidence team to come out? Also, can you run the plates? The registration card doesn't have the perp's name on it. If the vehicle is stolen, that'll be one more nail in the guy's coffin."

"No problem." Shane strode to his car, speaking into his radio as he went.

Tristan followed more slowly, eyeing the black sedan and the shattered window.

The guy who paid me...

That's what Butch had said.

Butch from Las Vegas, Nevada.

He dialed Las Vegas Metropolitan Police Department as he climbed back into the SUV. He left a message for Detective Smithfield explaining what had happened and asking for any information that might be pertinent to the case.

Hopefully the detective would get back to him quickly.

If Butch had been telling the truth, someone had paid him to kill Ariel. According to Ariel there was only one person she'd ever been afraid of, only one person who'd ever threatened her. Since he was dead, there had to be someone else. Someone that Ariel didn't know about or hadn't thought about.

Her ex-husband's girlfriend?

Could she be jealous of the baby Ariel was carrying? Jealous of Ariel for having what she couldn't?

It seemed far-fetched, but it was all Tristan had.

He climbed into his SUV, waved at Shane and headed back to the house.

As touchy as the subject was, he'd have to ask Ariel about it. If she knew the name of the girlfriend, Tristan could do a little checking, see if the woman was still in Las Vegas.

Whitney and Ryder were standing on the front porch with their dogs when Tristan pulled into his driveway. Whitney was shooting photos of the door frame while Ryder crouched a few feet away. He stood as Tristan approached.

"I heard you got the guy," he said without preamble.

"Eddie is transporting him. I plan to stop by the station after I check on—"

The door flew open, and Mia ran out, throwing her arms around Tristan the way she had when she was a little girl and he was her favorite big brother.

"I've been so worried." She sobbed into his shoulder. "Ms. Martin said you knew how to take care of yourself. She said you were going to come home to me, but Mom and Dad knew how to take care of themselves, and..."

Her voice trailed off, and she backed away, her cheeks damp with tears.

"It's okay, Mia. I'm okay." His heart ached for the pain he'd put her through, for the fear she'd experienced. "Ms. Martin is right. I do know how to take care of myself, and I'm always going to come home to you."

"You're a police officer, Tristan. You don't know if that's true."

"I trust that it is, because I'm committed to being around for as long as you need me, and I really believe that God is going to let me do that." He smoothed her hair, looked into her face. Sometimes he forgot how much she'd been through and how young she really was.

"Yeah? Well, if you're okay, then why is your arm bleeding?" She grabbed his hand and dragged him into the house. Jesse was there, pacing the living room, obviously sensing the tension. Sprinkles was following his lead, sprinting from one end of the room to the other.

There was no sign of Ariel.

"Where's Ms. Martin?" he asked as Mia used a towel to dab at the slice in his arm.

"She called Pastor Doug and Lauren, and they came to get her. I think she said she was getting her van and then going over to the parsonage. Now that the guy who was after her has been caught, she thought it would be safe to be there."

"I need to call the chief and have him run some patrols by her house," he said out loud. He wasn't happy that she'd left, and he wasn't convinced that she was safe. If Butch had been hired by someone, Ariel could still be in danger.

"Why? Ryder Hayes said the guy who was after her had been caught. He told Ms. Martin that he'd been arrested."

Tristan hooked Jesse to his leash. That was the lab's

signal that they were going to work, and the dog barked excitedly, tugging Tristan to the door. "Just to be on the safe side," he told his sister, opening the door and walking out into the warm afternoon. If the guy who'd shot at the house hadn't been caught, he wouldn't feel comfortable leaving Mia here. Still, he'd have one of the rookies drive by several times and keep a watch on the house.

Several neighbors were out in their yards, watching as Whitney and Ryder processed the scene. No doubt, the neighbors would stop by later to find out what had happened. He'd have to tell Mia not to open the door. He didn't want an overly dramatic version of the incident getting out to the public. Not after everything else that had been happening in town. The shooter was in police custody and no threat to the community.

He loaded Jesse into the SUV and drove back to the sedan, anxious to see if the lab alerted near the vehicle.

Shane was still at the scene, a county tow truck idling a few yards away, its driver scrolling through messages on his phone.

"That was quick," Shane said as Tristan let Jesse out of the SUV.

"Whitney and Ryder are processing the scene."

"Are your sister and Ariel okay?"

"Mia is fine. Ariel went back to the parsonage."

"You don't sound happy about that."

"Someone hired the guy who shot at us tonight. Until we find out who. Ariel still isn't safe. I already sent a text to the chief and asked him to run patrols on her street, but I'm not sure that will be enough."

"There isn't a whole lot more that can be done."

"That's not what I want to hear," Tristan said.

"I know, because we all think we can solve the world's problems, right? We all think that we can keep the people we care about safe. Sometimes, though, we can't. So, all we can do is our best and then pray that it's enough." He opened the back of his SUV and called for Bella.

"I need to head back to the station," Shane continued. "The chief said we'll impound the car, keep it for evidence retrieval. It was reported stolen in Las Vegas a few days ago, so we've got more paperwork to fill out and more charges to press. John will tow the car to the county impound lot once you're finished here." He motioned toward the tow-truck driver.

"Sounds good."

"I'll see you back at the station." Shane hopped in his SUV and drove away.

Tristan grabbed Jesse's vest, the dog whining excitedly as Tristan buckled him into it.

"Ready to work?" he asked, and Jesse let out a quick sharp bark.

They made their way down into the ditch, the lab tense with excitement, his tail high and still.

He knew what he was looking for, knew what he should be scenting.

"Find," Tristan said, and Jesse lunged toward the sedan, his excited barks ringing through the hot afternoon air.

TEN

$11{:}00$ p.m. Too late to be awake, but the baby was restless.

Or, maybe, Ariel was restless.

She'd been living in the parsonage for nearly a week, going to church, to work, to the police station.

How many times had she been *there*?

A dozen?

More?

First, she'd gone to look at mug shots of the guy who'd tried to kill her. Butch Harold wasn't anyone she'd ever seen before. She'd told Tristan that. She'd told Chief Jones that. She'd signed a paper that said it. After that, she'd been asked to file a report on the incident at the school. She'd been called in to discuss the fact that Tristan and his K-9 partner had found no sign of accelerants in the car Butch Harold had used. The police hadn't found any empty gas cans near the house, either. No evidence of smoke or fire on the clothes Butch had been wearing or any of the clothes they'd taken from a duffel in the back of his car.

Was she certain someone had been in the house with her? She'd been asked that question so many times, she'd begun to doubt her memory and her answer.

If Butch had been in the house, something of his should have had evidence of it. The police had found a bag of his clothes in the car he'd been driving. Not a hint of smoke or soot on any of them. Tristan has brought Jesse to the vehicle, had the dog sniff every inch of it. He'd found no hint of an accelerant, not even a trace of smoke or fire anywhere on the vehicle. If Butch hadn't been in the house, someone else had been there.

That's what Ariel thought about every night. It's what chased her from sound sleep and woke her in a cold sweat. She'd close her eyes, and she'd smell the smoke, she'd see the shadowy figure, hear his voice, feel the heat of the fire chasing her back up the stairs, and then she'd lie in bed, the baby kicking and wiggling, imagining the parsonage going up in flames. Tristan checked in with her every day. He called in the morning, stopped by the school in the afternoon and escorted her home. He'd done everything he could to make her feel safe, but she still felt afraid.

She walked across the large bedroom, the old floor-boards creaking beneath her feet. She needed to buy some throw rugs, a little bassinet for the baby to sleep in, a crib for the room across the hall. She'd been out twice since the fire, but replacing her phone and her bank cards had been a higher priority than stocking up on the things she'd need after the baby was born. She had managed to buy a couple of maternity outfits and a few small items that the baby would need, but at thirty-seven weeks, she was closing in on the home stretch. No one could predict how late or how early the baby would arrive, and sitting around brooding and worrying wasn't going to help Ariel prepare.

She opened the drawer in the bedside table and pulled out the notebook and pen she'd brought home from school. She'd make a list of what she needed, and she'd go out in the morning and spend the day shopping and preparing.

That would make her feel better about things.

She hoped, because she wasn't used to dwelling in her worries, and for the past few days that's what she felt like she'd been doing.

The truth was, she had nothing to be worried about. The attacks against her had stopped as soon as Butch Harold had been arrested. Since then, she hadn't felt hunted, she hadn't felt watched. There'd been no wiggling doorknobs in the middle of the night, no feeling that someone was standing just out of sight.

She'd walked to the school twice since the second shooting, and she hadn't felt anything but tired.

She was still afraid, though.

She kept running through the day of the fire, picturing the moment when she'd realized someone was in her house.

Not Mitch's girlfriend.

Ariel was certain the person was a man. Besides, Tristan had checked in on Mitch's girlfriend. A real estate broker in Las Vegas, Mora Hendricks had already found a new boyfriend. She insisted that she had nothing but goodwill for Ariel and the baby, and that she was disgusted with herself for ever getting involved with someone like Mitch.

Tristan hadn't been convinced of her remorse.

He'd told Ariel that Mora's new love interest was a married father of three with a healthy bank account and a lot of expensive things.

Ariel had been sorry for the guy's wife.

Eventually, she'd find out the truth, and her life would be turned upside down.

She'd told Tristan that.

He'd brought her a gift the next day. A huge sunflower

that he'd picked from an empty lot at the edge of town, a reminder that good things could grow from tough times.

That's what he'd told her.

She still had the sunflower sitting in a tall vase that she'd borrowed from Lauren. It was down in the kitchen, right next to the window he'd replaced earlier in the week. He'd been keeping Ariel informed, filling her in on all the details of the case while he worked on making the parsonage more secure.

While he'd put in new windows and doors, Ariel had tutored Mia. A fair exchange. That's how Tristan put it. Ariel thought she was getting the better end of the deal. She had a new alarm system, windows that would be very difficult to jimmy open and doors with bolts.

All Tristan had was a sister who was suddenly attending every class and getting an A on every assignment. He also had a sister who seemed happy to sit at Ariel's kitchen table every evening, her puppy in her lap as she worked on her assignments. Jesse was always near the back door, lying with his head on his paws, his golden eyes tracking Tristan's movements.

Ariel had cooked dinner every night.

For all three of them.

She'd also bought dog food and a bowl. Not for the dog that Tristan still wanted her to get. For Jesse and for Mia's puppy, Sprinkles. Every night, she filled the bowls, and the dogs ate, while she, Tristan and Mia shared a meal. They'd talk about their days and their plans, laughing and joking like a family.

It was starting to feel normal.

That scared Ariel more than she wanted to admit.

She'd made peace with her life. Mostly. She'd accepted her new situation. She had every intention of raising her daughter alone, because she was afraid of being hurt again, of being disappointed.

But, maybe, she didn't have to go it alone.

Maybe she could let Tristan into her life. He cared, he was always there, offering sincerity and humor and sweet words that made her feel like she mattered.

She scowled, carrying the notebook and pen down the stairs and into the kitchen. She flicked on the light and sat at the table. Mia had left a jacket on the back of the chair, and Ariel had a feeling that if she looked around, she'd find more evidence of the teen's presence. A small dog toy sat on the floor near the back door. A pencil lay on the counter. The house looked lived-in and happy. Exactly the way she'd always dreamed her home would be.

"Focus," she whispered, staring at the blank page in the notebook. "Baby stuff. What do we need?"

Blankets.

Baby wipes.

Onesies.

Someone knocked on the back door, the sound so startling, the pen flew from her hand and skittered across the floor. She tried to jump up from her seat, but her stomach bumped the table, nearly overturning it.

"Who's there?" she called as she yanked open a drawer and looked for a weapon. Lauren had lent her some utensils. Forks. Spoons. A few dull steak knives.

She grabbed one of those, edging toward the door, her heart beating frantically. She should have grabbed her cell phone from the bedside table. She could have called for help, because there was no way anyone she knew would be knocking on her door at this time of the night and the old rotary phone on the kitchen wall no longer worked.

"I said," she repeated, the knife clutched in her hand. "Who's there?"

"Mia." The voice was faint, but unmistakable.

Ariel threw open the bolt, tugged the teenager inside and slammed the door closed again.

"What are you doing outside at this time of night?" she nearly shouted, and Mia winced, her eyes red-rimmed, her cheeks damp. She had her backpack over her shoulders and what looked like slippers on her feet.

Had she run away from home?

She'd been crying, and that was enough to stop the reprimand that was on the tip of Ariel's tongue.

"What's wrong?" she said. "What happened?"

"Jenny and I had a big fight," the teen sobbed.

"You were at her house?"

"Tristan said I could spend the night. It was my reward for doing so well in school this week." Mia swiped tears from her cheeks. "Now it's all ruined, because Jenny won't listen to me."

"About what?"

"Anything!" Mia dropped into a chair, her legs splayed out under the table, her hair hanging limply around her shoulders. She looked pale and tired, her eyes deeply shadowed.

"There must be something specific that you want her to do."

Mia hesitated, then shrugged. "It doesn't matter what it is. If Jenny doesn't listen, we're not going to be friends. I told her that flat out."

"What do you want her to listen to you about? It must be important if you're willing to break up your friendship over it?"

Mia shrugged again, but didn't respond.

"Mia?" Ariel prodded. "Do you really think you should throw in the towel over a disagreement?"

"It's not a disagreement," Mia responded. "She's wrong."

"About?"

"She…" Mia began, then shook her head. "Nothing."

"If it's nothing, then it's not worth giving up the friendship over."

Mia wiped a few pieces of dog hair from her jeans, but didn't speak.

Ariel knew enough about teen girls to know that she and Mia could dance around the issue all night and never get to the root of it. Better to give Mia the chance to tell Ariel when she was ready. She'd come for that reason.

"Does Tristan know you're here?" she asked.

"He should."

"What does that mean?"

"I sent him a text when I saw your light. I told him I was going to see if you were awake because Jenny's grandmother's place is pretty far away, and my feet are tired from walking."

It wasn't that far, and Ariel was certain Mia had walked the distance on more than one occasion. She didn't point that out, though.

"He hasn't responded?"

"Of course not. Tristan is always too busy with his job to be bothered with me."

"That's unfair, Mia. I think you know it."

"I called him from Jenny's. I left him two messages saying I wanted to go home. He's always told me that if I ever have a problem, he'll drop everything to help me. But, he didn't return my calls, and he didn't show up. So, I walked. And, let me tell you, it's creepy out there at night." Her voice broke, and the tears started falling again.

"Maybe you should have waited a little longer," Ariel suggested. "Walking around by yourself this time of night probably wasn't the best idea."

"I know. I was just so mad. I've helped Jenny dozens of times, but I can't keep helping her. Not when…"

"What?" There was something going on between the two girls, and Ariel didn't think it was a petty disagreement. Both were strong-willed and smart. Both were creative and imaginative. They were like two sides of the same coin, and there had to have been a really serious problem for Mia to walk away from that.

"Have you ever kept a secret and then regretted it?" Mia asked, her dark eyes staring straight into Ariel's.

"Only once," she admitted.

"Did people find out? Did you get in trouble?"

"Yes, and no. But, I missed an opportunity to help someone I loved. I might even have missed an opportunity to save his life. I'd hate to see that happen with you."

"Are you talking about your husband?"

"No. My father. It's a long story. Maybe one day I'll tell it to you. For right now, I'll just say that my father was an alcoholic, and I helped him hide it. He drove off the road and flipped his car. He was killed instantly. For a long time, I wondered if I could have saved him. If I'd just said the right thing to the right person, if he might have gotten the help he needed."

"It wasn't your fault," Mia said, patting Ariel's arm. "You couldn't have known he would drink and drive."

"Maybe not, but I did keep his secret. I've always wished I hadn't."

"That stinks," Mia said quietly, and Ariel knew there was something she was holding back, something about Jenny maybe. A secret that she'd been keeping and didn't want to.

"Mia, it's hard to break a trust, but sometimes we have to. For the good of the person we love."

Mia bit her lip, her gaze jumping away.

"I—"

The doorbell rang, and Mia jumped up, obviously relieved by the interruption.

"I wonder if that's Tristan," she said, the words rushing out.

She ran from the kitchen. Ariel followed more slowly.

By the time she reached the living room, the front door was open and Tristan was standing in the entryway.

He didn't look happy, but he sure looked good, his hair just a little long, his eyes that deep brown that she couldn't seem to stop looking at.

He scanned the room, spotted his sister and walked straight to her, pulling her into his arms. "I'm glad you're okay, sis. I've been worried."

"You're not mad?" Mia mumbled against his shirt.

"I might be later. Right now, I'm just glad you found a safe place to wait for me." He patted her back, met Ariel's eyes. "Sorry about this, Ariel," he said, offering an apologetic smile.

"It's okay," Ariel responded. "And I was awake, so it's not like she pulled me out of bed for a visit."

"We still owe you an apology," he said, and Mia sighed.

"I apologize, Ms. Martin. Next time, maybe my brother will pick up his phone when I need him, and I won't have to bother you."

Tristan's jaw tightened, but he didn't rise to her bait. "I was in a meeting, Mia. If you'd given me a little more time, I'd have picked you up at Jenny's house."

"You won't have to worry about it anymore," Mia said. "Jenny and I are no longer friends. Which is exactly what you were hoping for. Happy now?" She burst into tears and ran from the house.

Tristan rubbed the back of his neck and sighed. "I guess I'd better go deal with that."

"Want me to talk to her?"

"You've already done more than your fair share to help our family, Ariel."

"I'm hearing yes," she said, and he laughed.

"I must be thinking really loudly, but I can't ask you to help. Not tonight. It's late, and you and the baby need to rest."

"The baby is wide-awake, and so am I."

"Too much on your mind?"

"I keep thinking about the fire and about the guy who was in the house with me. If it wasn't Butch Harold, who was it?"

She grabbed her purse from a hook near the door, not waiting for him to tell her again that he didn't need her help with Mia. Being with Tristan and his sister was a lot more appealing than pacing her room or writing a list of things she needed for the baby.

"I'm glad you brought that up. I planned to stop by tomorrow to discuss a few things with you," Tristan said, taking her arm as she walked out onto the porch.

"What things?"

"I spoke with Detective Smithfield again. I asked him to send me a copy of the medical examiner's report. I also asked for a copy of the accident report that was filed after Mitch's death."

The words left her cold, and she stopped short, turning to face him as they reached his SUV. "Why?"

"He was being investigated for insurance fraud."

"I know."

"He burned down five businesses."

She knew that, too. "What are you getting at, Tristan?"

He watched her for a moment, and she knew when he spoke, he was going to say something she didn't want to hear.

"Mitch's body couldn't be identified. Not by dental records. Not by fingerprints. He was so badly burned, that there was really nothing left for the medical examiner except DNA, and Mitch didn't have family."

"I know that, too."

"Do you know that the fire at the accident site burned so hot the metal on the car melted? If the fire department hadn't arrived when they did, there wouldn't have been anything but ashes left."

That was something she hadn't known. "You're getting at something, Tristan. Why not just tell me what it is?"

Why not?

Because Tristan didn't think it was something Ariel would want discussed in front of Mia. He didn't think she'd want to discuss it at all, but he'd made the calls, he'd read the reports and he couldn't shake the feeling that they were missing something really important.

Something really obvious.

Like the fact that her ex was an arsonist whose name had been tied to several insurance fraud cases. Mitch had been paid good money to make fires look like accidents, and he'd been mostly successful. If an insurance company hadn't gotten suspicious, if they hadn't hired a private investigator to check things out, Mitch probably would have continued to get paid for burning buildings to the ground.

Yeah. The guy had known his way around a fire.

To Tristan, it seemed a little too coincidental that he'd died in a car accident that had caused a fire that burned so hot it had melted metal and destroyed all but a small amount of DNA. The medical examiner had written a grim report. No fingerprints. No recognizable feature.

Teeth intact, but somehow Mitch's dental records had disappeared.

Another coincidence that Tristan didn't like.

"Tristan?" Ariel prodded, her face pale in the darkness. She hadn't been sleeping well. He'd noticed the dark circles under her eyes when he'd been at her house the previous day, noticed the narrow width of her shoulders, the thinness of her arms. She needed to eat and she needed to rest, but he doubted she'd do either until he gave her the answers that she wanted.

"How about we discuss it tomorrow?" he hedged, eyeing Mia through the dark glass of the SUV's back window.

She'd crossed her arms over her chest and closed her eyes. That didn't mean she wasn't listening to every word that was said.

"You don't want Mia to hear?"

"No, and I also don't want to keep you up any longer. You look tired, Ariel. That can't be good for the baby."

"It goes with the territory. I try to sleep. I can't. The baby keeps getting in the way." She touched her belly and smiled, but there was no humor in her eyes. She looked sad and a little worried, and he figured it would be a lot crueler to make her wait a few hours than to tell her something she might not want to hear.

"Tell you what," he said, opening the passenger-side door of the SUV. "If you really can't sleep, let's bring Mia home. We can talk after that."

She hesitated, then nodded. "All right, but I'll take my van. That way you won't have to drive me back."

"I'll end up following you back instead," he pointed out.

He opened the passenger door, and Ariel slid in without another word.

Mia was silent, too, her eyes still closed, her lips pressed together in an angry frown.

He'd have to talk to her, but first he needed to figure out the right thing to say. Not the snide remark he'd almost made before she'd stormed out of the house. Not a cut on Jenny's character or a cheer of approval over the end of the girls' friendship.

That wasn't what Mia needed or wanted from him.

The problem was, he had no idea what the right words were. He had no idea what it felt like to be a teenage girl who'd just broken up with her best friend. He also had no idea how to take back all the unflattering things he'd said about Jenny. If he'd kept his mouth shut, his sympathy might have sounded sincere. As it was, he doubted Mia would ever believe he was sorry about the situation.

The fact was, he wasn't sure he *was* sorry.

Jenny was a bad influence, and she had been from day one. The incident at the feed store had been the culmination of that. He'd asked Mia about it, and she'd denied everything. No way would Jenny ever shoplift. She and Jenny had been playing around. Jenny wouldn't have walked out of the store with dog food that didn't belong to them. That's what she'd said, and he'd wanted to believe her. She'd been working so hard at school and at home, that he'd let it go.

But, it had still been in the back of his mind.

Especially when he'd agreed to let her spend the night with her best friend. The one who was no longer her best friend.

He glanced in the rearview mirror, eyed his sister's pale face.

"I really am sorry, Mia," he said, and she opened her eyes, looked straight into his. He saw his mother in her gaze. He saw his father in the abrupt shrug of her shoulders.

"It doesn't matter," she replied.

"Sure it does," Ariel cut in. "It hurts when there's tension in a friendship."

"It wasn't a friendship anyway." Mia closed her eyes again, and that was it. The end of the conversation.

"There are all different kinds of friendships," Ariel said. "Some are meant to last for decades. Some last just long enough for us to find our way through tough times."

"I haven't found myself anywhere but in trouble since Jenny and I met," Mia muttered.

She sounded pitiful.

She looked pitiful.

"You've had fun with her, right?" Ariel asked.

"I thought I was having fun. Now, I just think I wanted a friend and Jenny was there. I guess when you don't have any other option, you take what's offered."

"Jenny is a nice girl. She just doesn't have as many rules as other kids your ages." Ariel seemed determined to make Mia feel better. Tristan could have told her it was a wasted effort. He'd spent the past few months doing everything he could to help Mia adjust to Desert Valley and their lives there.

"Whatever," Mia muttered.

"Mia," Tristan warned, because he could see where the conversation was heading. If things went the way they usually did, Mia's "whatever" would turn into some kind of angry rant.

She must have decided to skip that step and go straight to sullen moping, because she didn't say another word as he drove through Desert Valley and pulled into their driveway.

She was out of the SUV like a shot, sprinting across the dark front yard, racing up the porch steps and digging in her backpack at the same time.

Probably looking for her keys.

"Mia!" he called, planning to caution her, tell her to take things a little more slowly.

Too late.

She tripped on one of the porch steps, her gangly body flying forward. She landed with a loud thump, her backpack flying out of her hands, the contents spilling everywhere.

Tristan was out of the car and up the stairs before Mia was back on her feet. He took her sister by the arm, helped her back up, his heart heavy as he looked into her face.

He was failing.

By a lot.

The tears, the sadness, the anger? He had no idea how to deal with any of them.

Ariel didn't seem to have the same problem.

She patted Mia's arm, not even a little awkwardly. "That was quite a fall. Are you okay?"

"No!" Mia wailed, grabbing at one of the books that had fallen from her pack.

She picked it up, then reached for a sheaf of papers. As she snatched it up, something small and white bounced across the porch. A marble? Tristan grabbed it, planning to toss it in Mia's backpack, then realized he wasn't holding a marble. He was holding a pearl earring. Clip-on.

It looked exactly like the one found in the evidence room.

He went cold.

"Where did this come from?" he demanded, his voice harsher than he'd intended.

Mia looked up from the papers she was shoving in her pack.

"What?"

"This." He held the earring in front of her face, and she frowned.

"How should I know?"

"What is it?" Ariel asked, her hands filled with books and papers.

"It's an earring, and it was in your bag, Mia. It had to be. How else would it have gotten on the porch?"

"I have no idea." Mia took the papers from Ariel, shoved them into her bag and stood. "It's not mine."

"It fell out of your bag," he repeated.

There was no other explanation.

He'd heard it skitter across the porch floor. He'd seen it tumbling away from the things that had fallen from her pack. It had been in the bag. It had fallen out.

Now, she was saying she had no idea what it was or how it had gotten there.

"I didn't put it in my bag." She hefted the bag onto her shoulder and scowled. "And, I didn't steal it. If that's what you're implying."

"I'm not implying anything. I'm asking very simple questions that you don't seem to be able to answer."

"I did answer. Maybe I just need to be a little more simple in my reply," she retorted. "I. Don't. Know."

She whirled away, stomping to the front door and unlocking it. Sprinkles barked excitedly as she pushed it open, and she lifted the puppy, cuddling him close as she disappeared inside.

"What's wrong?" Ariel asked, her gaze on the earring. "Do you think she took it from Jenny?"

"There was an incident at the station a few weeks ago. This is connected to it." He couldn't tell her anything more, and she didn't ask. Instead, she grabbed a sweater and a notebook that had fallen.

"What are you going to do?" she asked, and he could see the sympathy in her eyes and on her face.

She must have known how serious the situation was. She must have understood how much trouble Mia could be in.

"The only thing I can do," he responded. "I'm calling my chief."

ELEVEN

Mia was in trouble. The kind that tutoring couldn't get her out of. Ariel stood in the living room of Tristan's small home, waiting as he went to get his sister.

She couldn't hear what was said, but she'd heard enough of his conversation with Chief Jones to know that the earring Tristan had found might somehow be connected to Veronica Earnshaw's murder.

The police had been searching for the dog trainer's murderer for months. As far as Ariel knew, they had no leads. If the earring was one, Mia might be in even bigger trouble than Ariel thought.

She wanted to walk down the hall, see if she could do anything to help, but it wasn't her business, this wasn't her family, so she stayed where she was.

Jesse lumbered over, nosing at her hand, his velvety muzzle warm and soft.

"Hey, boy," she murmured, scratching him between the ears, her gaze on the hallway. Still not a sound. Whatever Tristan was saying to his sister, he was saying it quietly.

Finally, a door opened, and Tristan reappeared, his dark hair ruffled as if he'd run his hand through it several times. She wanted to smooth it down, tell him that everything would be okay, but he met her eyes, shook his head.

"I'm sorry, Ariel. We're going to have to talk another time. I've got to bring Mia to the station."

"That doesn't sound good."

"It isn't, and if she doesn't start talking, it will be even worse."

"She's fourteen, getting anything out of girls that age is difficult."

"Unfortunately, this isn't a good time for her teenage angst to be at full throttle. She's going to be in serious trouble if she doesn't open her mouth and speak up."

"I spoke up," Mia grumbled, stepping into the hall. She'd changed into dark jeans and an oversize sweatshirt. Despite her height and the hint of makeup around her eyes, she looked like a little kid, her hair pulled back into a high ponytail, her cheeks pink with anger or frustration.

"You didn't say anything that would help your case, Mia," Tristan said, smoothing his hair. He looked a hundred times more frustrated than his sister, but he kept his tone even, his expression neutral. "We'll drive Ms. Martin home, and then I'll take you to speak with the chief."

"Tristan, I didn't do anything wrong. I've never ever seen that earring before. That's the honest truth." Mia sounded desperate.

"Whether you did or not doesn't matter. You have to talk to Chief Jones," he responded, hooking Jesse to a leash and leading him outside.

Ariel followed, leaving the door cracked open, the sound of Mia's muttered response to her brother drifting out into the balmy night.

He heard.

She could see the tension in his shoulders, the hint of anger in his face.

"Is there anything I can do to help?" she asked, and despite herself, despite every warning in her head that told her that getting too close to Tristan and his sister would be a mistake, she touched his shoulder, her hand just skimming the warm fabric of his cotton shirt.

"I don't think there's anything anyone can do to help," he responded, his eyes dark in the porch light.

"How much trouble is she in?"

"It depends on how much she hasn't told me." He pulled a plastic bag from his pocket. He'd dropped the earring into it while he was speaking with Chief Jones.

"You're assuming that she hasn't told you everything."

"Aren't you? You've seen how my sister is. She keeps secrets if she thinks it will keep her out of trouble." he said, his focus on the earring.

"That maybe be true, but she's been trying the past week."

"Trying to what? Convince me that she's staying out of trouble while she's knee-deep in it?" He shoved the earring back into his pocket and sighed.

"She's not a bad kid, Tristan. She's just a kid," she reminded him. "They make mistakes. That doesn't mean they'll keep making them."

"Tell that to the chief, because he's going to want an explanation for how my sister got that earring, and her silence isn't going to be enough of an answer."

"Okay," she said, and he raised an eyebrow in question.

"Okay what?"

"I'll talk to Chief Jones. I'll tell him that Mia is a good kid."

He smiled, just a quick curve of the lips. "I appreciate the offer, but you need to get home."

"And you don't think my opinion is going to help?"

"We've had a lot of crime in Desert Valley recently, Ariel. Everyone is on edge."

"Including your sister. Maybe this time she needs more

than her brother standing in her corner fighting for her. Maybe she'd like her teacher to be doing the same."

"And maybe she'd like people to stop talking about her like she's not old enough to make her own decisions," Mia blurted out from behind the door. Obviously, she'd been listening.

"Since you're standing right here—" Tristan opened the door, took his sister's arm "—we may as well get going."

"I'd rather not."

"I already explained that you don't have a choice."

"Well, then. I want Ms. Martin to come." She grabbed Ariel's arm.

"I don't think—" Tristan began.

"That I have a choice in that, either?" Mia nearly spat the words. "Then what do I have a choice in? You didn't let me stay where I had friends. You didn't let me decide to attend high school with all the people I've known my whole life. You made me go to a new church in a new town filled with a bunch of stuck-up brats who have all kinds of money and no sense. If Mom and Dad knew how unhappy I was, they'd hate you!"

She released Ariel's wrist and stomped down the stairs, climbed into the SUV and slammed the door.

"Wow," Tristan muttered, and Ariel's heart ached for him.

He was doing the best he could in a difficult situation, but sometimes a person's best wasn't enough to change things. She'd learned that the hard way.

"You've done everything you can to make her happy," she said quietly, and he met her eyes, shook his head.

"Obviously not."

"She's angry. She'll feel differently in an hour."

"She's been feeling this way for months. That's why

she's doing so poorly in school. It's why she hasn't made more friends. It's why she hangs out with Jenny. She wants what she used to have. I took all of it from her, and she wants to make sure I know just how much she's suffering."

"You didn't take her mother and father. That's what she misses the most and that's what she wants the most."

"If I could bring them back, I would. She's not the only one who misses them, but I'm an adult, she's a kid, and I do understand how hard things are for her. What I don't understand is all the trouble she keeps getting into. She was always such a great kid. Never any kind of trouble for my parents. She and I always got along great. She was an ace student. I should never have brought her here."

He turned away, and she knew the conversation was over, that he didn't want to say anything else about his sister or their struggles. She could have honored that, kept her mouth shut, kept her thoughts to herself, but she knew how it felt to fail. She knew the sick churning feeling of regret.

She followed him, catching his arm when he would have opened the door to the SUV. "You made the best decision you could," she said. "Don't waste your time second-guessing yourself."

"It's human nature to doubt our decisions," he responded. "Especially when everything we're working to preserve is falling apart. If something happens to Mia because I moved her here, I'll never forgive myself."

That was another thing Ariel understood—how hard it was to forgive yourself. Forgiving others was so much easier.

"After my husband filed for divorce," she said, the words ringing out into the quiet night. "I was angrier at myself than I was at him. I thought that if I'd made a better decision, if I'd been more careful about the guy I'd chosen, if I'd worked just a little harder or done just a little more, things would have turned out differently."

"Your husband was a liar, a thief and a cheat, Ariel. That had absolutely nothing to do with you."

"Maybe not, but now I'm going to be raising my daughter alone. She's going to have a mother who loves her, but she won't have a father."

"You don't have raise her alone," he said simply, and she knew there was a question in the words, knew that he was asking if he might be included in her life and the baby's.

"Tristan," she began, and he held up a hand, stopping her words.

"I'm not asking you to offer your undying affection, Ariel. I'm just asking you to think about letting me into your life. Me and Mia. We're kind of a package deal." He smiled, and she found herself smiling in return.

He did that to her, made her feel like everything was going to be okay, like the things that seemed so overwhelming, so insurmountable, were tiny little blips on the radar of her life.

"It's a nice idea, Tristan."

"But?"

"No buts. Our friendship is new, and neither of us can know where it's going to lead."

Maybe not.

Probably not.

Tristan wasn't even sure what the next day was going to bring. He couldn't say for sure where his relationship with Ariel was going to lead.

He wanted to try, though.

He wanted to offer her the support she deserved. "We

can know that we'll try, and you can know that I'll always be there for the baby. No matter what happens between us."

She didn't respond.

He hadn't expected her to.

She'd been through too much. She'd been betrayed and hurt, and he was asking her to put that aside, believe that something she'd stopped believing in was possible.

He could have pushed her for an answer.

He could have told her that they were heading in a direction together, whether either of them wanted to or not. Instead, he leaned toward her, brushed her lips with his. Just a gentle touch, one that gave her a glimpse into his heart.

He didn't care that Mia was in the car, didn't care that she might ask questions. He and Ariel had come too far together, and he wasn't willing to turn away from her.

"We have time," he said. "And I'm willing to wait."

He opened her door and helped her into the seat. Her stomach seemed to be growing a little more every day, her small-boned frame barely able to accommodate the baby. The bigger her stomach got, the thinner her arms and legs seemed to be, the gaunter her face.

That worried him.

"You need to eat more," he said, and she laughed shakily.

"That was a quick change of subject."

"You didn't seem excited about the other one. I thought I'd switch things up."

"I'm eating." She patted her belly. "But I can't fit much in anymore. The kid is taking up more than her fair share of space."

"You need to pop that little girl out," Mia said absently,

her head bent over her cell phone. Hopefully, she wasn't texting Jenny.

He wouldn't put it past her, and he almost warned her to put the phone away and not give Jenny any information about the earring or the fact that they were heading to the police station.

Sure, Mia had said Jenny wasn't her friend anymore, but that meant nothing.

Knowing her, she'd tell Jenny even more, if he warned her against it. Just to spite him, because that's what she lived for.

Not nice.

The words whispered through his mind, and they sounded just like his mother's. She'd said that to him when he was a kid, poking fun at another child or one of his teachers.

"Not nice, Tristan. You never know where someone has come from or what they've been through. You might be laughing at a person who's got nothing but sorrow in his heart."

It had taken him a few years to understand what she'd meant. He'd finally gotten it when he'd heard a group of his friends laughing at Lyle Henry. The kid had holes in his shoes and smelled like cigarette smoke. Everyone knew that his mother had died when he was six, and the teachers made certain that he wasn't picked on. Not to his face. Behind his back, kids whispered, they talked and they laughed.

Tristan had often joined in. Childish jokes. Harmless fun. Until he'd heard his friends laughing and had seen Lyle just a few feet away, cheeks red, eyes lowered. He'd heard every word. The next day, he hadn't come to school. The day after that, he'd been absent, too. By the end of a week, Tristan had felt bad enough to ride his bike to

Lyle's house, knock on a front door that had peeling paint and splintered wood. An old man had opened the door, a cigarette dangling from his lips, the stench of it drifting in the air. When Tristan asked for Lyle, the guy had told him to come in.

The place had been filthy, the carpets layered with grime, the walls dingy from smoke. Lyle had shuffled down steep stairs, hitching up pants that were too big, his hair cut in some awful style that Tristan had known the other kids would make fun of.

Right on the wall behind him, there was a picture of a woman with a pale, pretty face. Next to her, a smaller, younger version of Lyle. In the picture, he was clean, his hair nice, his smile happy. In the picture, he'd looked like a normal average kid. Like Tristan or any one of his friends.

And, that's when Tristan had known just how cruel he'd been, just how wrong.

He didn't want to make the same mistake with his sister.

She hid her sorrow well, but she was still feeling the loss of their parents. He'd be a fool to ignore that, to not take into account how much it impacted her actions.

He settled Jesse into his crate, slid into the driver's seat, the tension in the vehicle thick and uncomfortable.

There were a lot of things Tristan could have said, a lot of questions he wanted to ask. Somehow, the match to the earring that had been found in the evidence room had been in Mia's bag. There had to be a reason for that, and there had to be an explanation.

Mia had insisted she had no idea.

He could choose to believe her, choose to stand by and support her, or he could choose to believe she was lying. Ariel had been right when she'd said that Mia was a good kid. She'd made mistakes, but she'd been working to correct them.

He shifted, turning so he could look at his sister, see their parents in her face.

"Mia," he said, and she stared him down, mutiny in her eyes. "Before you talk to the chief, I want you to know something."

"That you think I'm a loser?" she muttered, tears in her eyes.

"That I believe you. We'll figure out how the earring got in your backpack. *I'll* figure it out. All you have to do is keep moving in the direction you've been going. Good grades. Good attitude."

He turned away before she could respond, but caught the look of surprise on her face. He shoved the keys in the ignition and starting the SUV.

Chief Jones was waiting for them. He was pretty certain several other members of the K-9 team would be at the station. A match to the earring they'd found in the evidence room—near where the Veronica Earnshaw evidence box *should* have been—was something they'd all been waiting on. If they could figure out where it had come from, they might just find Veronica's killer.

He backed out of the driveway, surprised when Ariel leaned close, her lips almost touching his ear, as she whispered, "Good job."

"We'll see," he responded, and she chuckled.

"We already saw." She backed away, shifted so that she was looking out her window. "I've been thinking about what you said. About Mitch and the car accident he was in."

Obviously, she didn't want to wait to have their discussion. He glanced in the review mirror. Mia had ear-

buds in and was bopping around to some song or another.
"What about it?"

"I never understood why Mitch was so determined that
I not have the baby. Even after we got divorced. It made
no sense. He wasn't going to have any legal obligation.
I'd signed papers that released him of his financial re-
sponsibilities, but he wouldn't let it go."

"I think we've established that your ex wasn't a very
moral guy. He wanted his freedom."

"From me? From the baby? He had it."

True. Tristan had seen the legal documents. "Maybe
he was motivated by spite," he suggested. "He didn't want
you to be happy. Or…"

He stopped before he said it. The thing that had been
nudging the back of his mind, the idea that he couldn't
quite shake.

"What?" she asked, her voice tight.

She knew what he was thinking.

He was almost positive that she did.

"Like I said before," he responded, "it's convenient
that there was no way to identify Mitch's body. It was
his car. His gender. His height. Body type. Those things
all match, but the only way to know for sure would be to
compare his DNA with a relative's."

That was it.

He didn't say anything else, just let the words hang
there.

They were nearing the police station when Ariel finally spoke, her voice just loud enough to be heard above
the soft rumble of the engine. "The baby is his only living relative."

"I know."

"If he were alive, he'd want to start again, right? Doing
what he's been doing to make money?" she continued

as if he hadn't spoken. "Or maybe living off money he's made from other schemes. The police were investigating several arsons, but had only been able to tie him to five. He could have made a boatload of money and socked it away overseas."

"He was smart enough to do that, and probably greedy enough to keep working his angle, making money off insurance fraud," Tristan agreed. He'd read up on the guy, talked to a few people who'd worked with him. Most people hadn't been fond of him, but they'd all agreed he was smart and he knew how to work any system to his advantage.

"He's also smart enough to know that the police might get suspicious if there are more fires, ones that match his MO." She tapped her fingers against her thigh. "They might want to check the baby's DNA, see if it matches the DNA extracted from the victim of the car accident. DNA from new crime scenes, too. If it did, they'd be hunting him down, and they'd find him. He would have to know that. If he were alive," she said the last part so quietly he almost didn't hear.

It was what he'd been thinking, though, what he'd been worrying about.

If Mitch was alive, that would explain everything.

If he was alive, that would give Butch Harold a really good reason to keep his mouth shut about the person who'd paid him to kill Ariel. A guy who wanted to get rid of his own child wouldn't hesitate to kill a hired lackey.

It was something Tristan planned to discuss with Chief Jones.

He touched Ariel's hand, found himself linking fingers with her, offering comfort that he knew she needed. She needed more than comfort, though. She needed her ex found, and maybe, too, she needed to know just how much Tristan cared.

"It's going to be okay, Ariel. I'm going to figure out what's going on. If your ex is alive, I'm going to make sure he doesn't get anywhere close to you."

She squeezed his hand in acknowledgment but didn't speak as they pulled up in front on of the police station and parked beneath a glowing street light.

TWELVE

Mitch. Alive.

Those two words ran through Ariel's head over and over again, chilling her blood and making her stomach churn. She tried to drown them out by listening to the K-9 officers who were gathered in a conference room nearby. She could hear bits and pieces of their conversation, but not enough to be interesting and not enough to drive those words out of her head.

Mitch.

Alive.

It had never occurred to her before. She'd never even considered the fact that he might not have died in the accident, that someone else might have been behind the wheel of the vehicle.

If it was true, if Mitch had faked his death, everything else made sense. The eerie feeling that she was being watched, the odd sense that she wasn't alone.

She shivered, pacing across the small room Tristan had left her in. He'd said he'd be back soon. That had been a half hour ago. She hadn't heard from him or anyone else since.

Obviously, the interview with Mia wasn't going well. The teenager had secrets, but Ariel didn't think the earring had anything to do with them. She'd looked genuinely surprised to see it, genuinely confused as to who it might belong to.

She'd also seemed stunned when Tristan had told her that he believed her, that he'd figure things out.

Tristan was a good guy, the kind of guy that Ariel had been looking for when she'd found Mitch.

"You were such a fool," she muttered.

"What's that?" Tristan asked, his voice so surprising that she startled, nearly tipping over as she whirled to face him.

He stood in the open doorway, his eyes shadowed, his jaw covered with stubble.

"Just talking to myself," she responded, her cheeks hot. "How's everything going?"

"The way I expected. Mia is insisting that she knows nothing about the earring."

"I don't think she does."

"Me, neither. The problem is, I'm sure she's hiding something. She's nervous and edgy, and it's making all of us suspicious."

"Including you?"

"Something is going on with her, Ariel. I just wish I knew what." He ran a hand down his jaw, shook his head. "But, I don't want to keep you here any longer. We're all taking a ten-minute break, so I can give you a ride home. I want to leave Jesse at your place—if anyone comes near your house, he'll alert you. The moment he does, call me and 911." He patted the lab's head and was rewarded with what Ariel was certain was a doggy smile.

Ariel nodded. "I don't mind staying, though, Tristan. I did tell Mia that I'd be here for her, and I'd like to at least say goodbye before I abandon her."

"I don't think it counts as abandoning her when I'm

forcing you to go." He offered a weary smile. "For the baby's sake, you really do need to rest, Ariel."

He was right.

She knew it, but the thought of going home to the empty house, even with Jesse, made her sad.

"All right. I'll leave, but tell Mia—"

Someone knocked on the doorjamb, and secretary Carrie Dunleavy walked in. She smiled shyly, holding up two disposable cups. "Coffee, Tristan?" she asked, holding one toward him.

"Thanks, Carrie. You're a gem."

She blushed and held the other cup out to Ariel.

"This is hot chocolate. Lots of real milk and just a little chocolate. I didn't think you'd want a lot of caffeine." Her gaze dropped to Ariel's stomach, and she blushed again.

"That's really thoughtful of you," Ariel said, taking the cup and smiling at the woman. Ariel appreciated how kind Carrie had been to Mia when Tristan had needed a safe place to leave the girl the other day.

"Very," Tristan added. "Especially considering that your shift ended hours ago. Did Chief Jones call you back in?"

"No." Carrie's blush deepened, her skin suddenly the color of a ripe tomato. "I was out on my way home and saw a few of the K-9 officers walking across the parking lot. That seemed odd, so I decided to stop in and see if I could assist anyone. I was really sorry to hear that your sister had been taken in for questioning."

Tristan frowned. Ariel had the feeling he didn't like word of that spreading. "Who told you that?"

Carrie bit her lip. "Ellen mentioned it. But, she didn't say questioning," she hurried to add, clearly hoping to make Tristan feel better. "She just said that you'd brought

Mia in to speak with Chief Jones. Did something happen? Is Mia okay?"

"She seems to be," Tristan responded kindly, but he was still frowning, his gaze focused on Carrie.

"Great. Good. I'm going to see if anyone else wants coffee."

"Or, you could go home. It's past midnight," Tristan pointed out. "You're working the early shift, right?"

"I'm a night owl," Carrie said with a nervous laugh. "I don't mind being out until the wee hours of the morning. I'll just check in with the chief and see if he needs anything."

She scurried from the room.

"Carrie seems very dedicated to the police department," Ariel said, sipping the sweet chocolate.

"Yeah." He frowned.

"What's wrong?"

"I don't know. Just something at the back of my mind that I can't quite catch hold of. Every time I see Carrie, I think there's something I'm not putting my finger on, then she runs off and it's gone. I think I'll have a chat with her later. See if I can figure it out. Come on. Let's get out of here." He took her arm, his fingers caressing the inside of her elbow, and for a moment she was back at the house, his lips brushings hers, a million butterflies taking flight in her stomach.

She'd been trying to forget about the kiss, trying to tell herself it had meant nothing, but she'd known it meant way more than that. She'd felt it to her soul, the gentleness of the touch, the promise in it.

"I've been thinking about your ex," Tristan said as he led her into the hall.

The words were a splash of ice water in the face. "What about him?"

"He was a criminal. A liar. A cheat."

"No need for the reminder, Tristan. I'm very aware of what he was."

He nodded, eyes filled with concern and compassion. "I know, and I'm sorry. The thing is, Mitch was also a fool, Ariel. He didn't value what he had. If I were ever in his position, if I ever had the love of a woman like you, I would know exactly how blessed I was."

"I—" she began, not sure what she was going to say.

"Tristan!" Mia called, her voice ringing through the hallway, her feet tapping against the floor as she raced toward them. Her eyes were wide with fear, her face leeched of color. She was crying again. Silent tears that streamed down her face.

"What happened, Mia?" Tristan pulled her into his arms, patting her back the way he probably had when she was a tiny kid and he was an awkward teenager.

"Carrie said you'd left me."

"No!" Carrie called, hurrying toward them. "You misunderstood, Mia. I didn't say he'd left you. I said, he'd left."

"Same thing!" Mia cried.

"What's going on out here?" Chief Jones asked, stepping into the hall, Ellen Foxcroft and Ryder Hayes and their K-9 partners beside him. "Mia, I thought we agreed that you'd stay in the interview room and wait while I made a phone call."

"I was going to, but Carrie—"

"I didn't say that your brother left you," Carrie snapped, the harsh tone so surprising that everyone went silent. "Sorry," Carrie mumbled. "I…just. That's not what I said."

Mia's face crumpled. "You *were* going to leave me,

weren't you, Tristan? Because I've been such a brat. You were going to let them take me off to juvenile hall."

"Hon," Chief Jones said, his voice gentle. "We weren't going to take you anywhere. We just wanted the truth."

"I told you the truth!" she cried. "But not about everything. I'm really sorry, Tristan. I should have told you from the very beginning."

"Told me what?" Tristan looked as confused as Ariel felt, his dark eyes jumping from his sister to Chief Jones and then settling on Ariel.

"Help me?" he mouthed, and she moved a little closer, touched Mia's shoulder.

"Mia, what's going on? You're carrying too big a burden for someone so young, and it's making you do all kinds of things you normally wouldn't. If you share the weight of it with us, we can help."

Mia wiped tears from her cheeks and took a shuddering breath. "I just don't want to get Jenny in trouble. She didn't mean any harm."

"Didn't mean any harm when she did what?" Tristan asked,

"That puppy that went missing from the training center the night the trainer was murdered? The one that everyone is looking for? Jenny found it, and she took it to her grandmother's house. She's been keeping it in her grandmother's barn. That's what we were fighting about tonight. I told her she had to turn the puppy back over to the training center, and she said she wasn't going to do it."

For a moment, everyone was silent, then they were all talking at once. Chief Jones telling Tristan that they needed to get to the Gilmores' house. Ellen saying that she'd call the K-9 training center and get the microchip reader. Ryder speaking on his radio, talking to another K-9 officer.

Ariel could sense the excitement, the anxiety, and she took Mia's hand, starting to lead her away from the group.

"Hang on for a minute, okay?" Tristan said, snagging Ariel's wrist, his fingers warm, his touch light. He was looking into her eyes, and she couldn't stop looking back, seeing the intensity in the blue of his gaze.

"Should we call Jenny's grandmother?" Ellen asked, and whatever seemed to be between Ariel and Tristan disappeared. "Let her know we're on the way?"

"And give Jenny a chance to hide the puppy?" Ryder responded. "I don't think so."

"Me, neither," Chief Jones agreed. "Tristan and Ryder, why don't the two of you head to Jenny's place? Ellen, want to call the new trainer? Ask Sophie to bring the microchip scanner here? We'll meet in my office ASAP and get the chip read. Hopefully, we'll get the answer we're looking for."

"Answer to what?" Ariel asked.

"The question of who murdered Veronica Earnshaw," Chief Jones answered grimly. "Carrie, can you…"

His voice trailed off. "Where did she go?"

"Probably too much action for her," Ryder commented. "You know how she is. She's quiet, and she doesn't like a lot of commotion. She'll turn back up eventually. She always does. Let's go get that puppy, Tristan."

Getting the puppy was Tristan's first priority. Otherwise, he'd have gone looking for Carrie. There was something he was missing about her, and he wanted to know what it was.

First, though, they had to get the puppy and have the microchip scanned. If Veronica had been able to leave a clue about her murderer, that's where it would be.

"All right. Let's go," he said, as anxious as Ryder was to get going.

"You can't just go barging in on them," Mia protested. "Jenny's grandmother is old. She'll freak out and have a heart attack and die, then Jenny will never forgive me!"

"We can't wait, Mia," Tristan responded as patiently as he could.

He was angry, and he thought he had a good reason to be. Mia had lied. She'd helped her friend keep a puppy that didn't belong to her—a puppy the police had been searching for for months now. He thought about the empty dog food bag, the incident at the feed store. It all made sense now. Mia wouldn't have wanted the puppy to go hungry. She'd have made sure it had food, but she would have drawn the line at stealing. She'd probably been trying to convince Jenny to put the food back when Lauren spotted them.

"Tristan, seriously, you have to listen to me. Jenny loves that puppy. She's going to be heartbroken if you take it."

"Sweetie," Ellen said gently. "My mother donated the puppies to the training center, and that's who they belong to. No matter how much your friend loves the puppy, it's not hers."

"But—"

"You know," Ariel broke in, the cup of chocolate still in her hand. It made him think of Carrie again, of that niggling thing that he couldn't quite pull from his mind. "It might be best if a woman went with you, a woman who's not a police officer. And someone Jenny's grandmother knows. I've been out there a couple of times to visit. She might respond better to me than to anyone else."

No, Tristan was going to say, because she looked exhausted, and he wanted to ask Ellen to drop her off at her place.

The chief had other ideas. He nodded. "That's a good idea, Ariel. I sure appreciate your help in the matter."

"It's no problem. I'd hate for Ms. Gilmore to get confused or upset about the situation. She might be afraid that you're going to bring Jenny to juvenile detention, but I'm sure that's not your plan."

It wasn't a question, but the chief shook his head. "It's not. We want the puppy back, and I'm sure we'll have a few things to say to Jenny, but if she's been taking good care of the puppy, we may be able to just let it go. We'll have to discuss it later."

"She is taking good care of the puppy," Mia said earnestly.

"I'm sure," Ariel responded. "She's a good kid. She's made a childish mistake, but I think we can all understand it. She found the puppy and then couldn't bear to give it back. What she did was wrong—she knew the police were looking for him, but I do hope she can pay for her crime by doing community service, perhaps volunteering at the training center. Since she's only fourteen, I'd be happy to accompany her."

Tristan might not have been so forgiving, but Mia looked so relieved and Ariel made a good case. He kept his mouth shut.

"Ellen, is there any chance you can drop my sister off at our place?" he asked.

"I don't want to go home. Jenny is my friend—"

"That's not what you said an hour ago," Tristan pointed out and was rewarded with a scowl.

"I still like Jenny. Even if we aren't friends. I don't want her to get in trouble because of me."

"If she's in trouble, it's because of her actions and it

has nothing to do with you," Ariel said gently. "Now, how about you do what your brother wants without arguing? The sooner we get this over with, the sooner Jenny can make amends and move on."

It seemed to be the right thing to say.

Mia sighed. "All right. Fine. I'll go home."

"And stay there?" Tristan prodded.

"That, too."

Good. That was what he wanted to hear. The last thing he needed was his sister running to rescue her friend.

Her friend who'd been hiding the puppy the team had been searching for.

"Hard to believe, isn't it?" Ryder asked as Ellen led Mia away.

"That a teenage girl could fall in love with a puppy?" Ariel responded before Tristan could. "Not really. I've seen the picture of the German shepherd puppy. He's every kid's perfect dog."

"That two teenage girls could keep a puppy hidden for so long. Especially when an entire town was looking for it," Ryder said.

"The Gilmores are pretty far outside town," Tristan said, calling to Jesse and then heading down the hall. He was anxious to get a look at the puppy Jenny was keeping. It was possible Mia was mistaken, that Jenny had found some other dog.

It was possible, but he didn't think she *was* mistaken.

The timing was too perfect, the change in Mia's attitude coinciding with Veronica's murder, the missing puppy, the other crimes that had been happening in town. He should have seen the connection sooner, but he'd been so caught up in the investigation, so certain that his sister was just rebelling because she didn't like Desert Valley, that he hadn't looked any further than that for an explanation of her behavior.

"There is no man so blind as the one who will not see," he muttered as he opened the door to his SUV and helped Ariel in.

"What's that?" she asked, her mouth curved in a half smile.

"Just thinking that I should have realized what my sister was hiding. Now that she's told me the truth, it seems pretty obvious. Dog food missing. A sudden interest in all things puppy."

"Lots of girls that age love animals."

"Maybe so, but—"

"Don't waste time looking back, Tristan. Take it from someone who's been there and done that—it won't change anything. All it can possibly do is make you doubt yourself."

"Is that what you've been doing?" he asked as he pulled out of the parking lot. "Doubting yourself?"

"Absolutely," she responded without hesitation. "I question everything I think, every decision I make, because of Mitch."

"Maybe we both need to be a little kinder to ourselves," he said.

"Okay. You first."

That made him laugh. A surprise, because he wasn't in a laughing kind of mood. If Mia was right about the puppy, the key to finding Veronica's murderer had been right under his nose for months.

Right under his nose. Living in his house. Lying every day.

He frowned, glancing in his rearview mirror. Ryder was right behind him, his SUV's strobe lights on. He was as anxious to find the truth as Tristan. Maybe even more so. Tristan had been hoping to find answers to his friend Mike's death. He hadn't believed the rookie K-9 officer's fall down the stairs was an accident, and he'd been determined to learn the truth.

There'd been no clues, though. No hint that Mike hadn't just taken a hard fall down the steps.

Ryder's wife *had* been murdered, though. She'd been shot. Just like Veronica. Was it possible that finding Veronica's murderer would lead them to Melanie's? That's what the team was hoping for, and they were about to find out.

The Gilmores' farmhouse was just ahead, the old structure a hulking black shadow against the dark sky. There were no lights on in the house, just a lone bulb glowing from the porch.

Tristan parked the SUV and climbed out, opening the back hatch for Jesse. Ariel was out of the vehicle before he got to her door, her face pale in the moonlight.

"I feel bad waking them up," she whispered as Ryder got out of his car and released his K-9 partner from the back.

"We don't have a choice. If the puppy is here, we need to find it." Tristan called Jesse to heel and headed up the rickety porch stairs. The place had seen better days, but he knew Ms. Gilmore did her best. On a limited income, with limited health and energy, she was raising a difficult teenager.

He knocked on the door and thought he heard a puppy barking somewhere in the distance.

The old barn?

That's where Mia said it would be.

"How about I go over to the barn and take a look?" Ryder suggested, Titus sniffing the ground beside him. The dog scented something.

"Let's both—"

The door creaked open, and an old woman appeared, her white hair wild around her head, her wrinkled face slack with surprise. "What in the world is going on out here? My granddaughter said there were police cars outside, and I guess she was right."

"Actually, Ms. Gilmore," Ariel said, smiling kindly at the older woman. "We're here to speak with Jenny. I'm her teacher, Ariel—"

"Martin. I'm old. Not senile. What has that girl done now?" The older woman sighed, opening the door wider and gesturing for them to enter. "Jenny!" she called.

There was no answer, and Tristan met Ryder's eyes.

"The barn?" he suggested.

"I think so," Ryder replied as Titus began to bark frantically, pulling at the lead and lunging toward the still-open door. A shadow was moving near the edge of the driveway, darting through sparse trees and heading toward a distant outbuilding.

"Let's go," Tristan commanded, running back outside with Jesse.

He didn't release the dog, just let him have the lead as they raced toward the retreating figure.

THIRTEEN

Tristan and Ryder were gone just long enough for Ariel to explain the situation to Ms. Gilmore. The older woman seemed more annoyed than angry, her eyes red-rimmed with fatigue as she puttered around the kitchen, putting on a teakettle, her old housecoat at odds with her perfectly styled hair. She had clearly rushed to powder her face before she'd answered the door. There were specks of powder on her cheeks and a dusting of it across her nose. She'd tried for mascara, and it had smeared, dots of it staining her cheeks. She had rings on every finger. Earrings on both ears. One pearl. One gold stud. Clip-ons. One of them dangling precariously.

"I just don't understand that girl at all," Ms. Gilmore said, pouring hot water over a tea bag and handing Ariel a cup. "I've tried so hard to instill good values in her, and then she up and does something like this. Stealing a dog? It's just unconscionable."

"She might not have known she was stealing it, Ms. Gilmore," Ariel said, shouting a bit since the woman was hard of hearing. "When she first found it, she might have thought it was a stray."

"When she first found it, yes, but after that, there was no excuse. And, I'm sure her sweet little friend was telling her that." She shook her head, white curls bouncing around her head, the loose earring flopping around. "I suppose I'm going to have to bring her to that counselor she was seeing after her mother died. She's in the next town over, though, and it's a long drive at my age. Maybe—"

Whatever she was going to say was cut off by the sound of a door opening, dogs barking, men talking and a girl yelling very loudly, "It's not fair! Sparkle is mine. I found him, and you can't just take him away."

"I guess that is my cue to do something," Ms. Gilmore murmured, hurrying out into the foyer.

Ariel followed.

Tristan and Ryder were there, Jenny standing between them with a big German shepherd puppy sitting at her feet. It was a handsome dog, big feet and young thin body. Calm. Not barking or jumping. As a matter of fact, it looked like a younger, thinner version of a few K-9 dogs she'd seen.

"Hi, Jenny," Ariel said, and the teen's eyes widened.

"What are you doing here?"

"Is that any way to talk to your teacher?" Ms. Gilmore snapped, marching over to her granddaughter, her blue eyes blazing. "I cannot believe that you've caused this ruckus, Jenny Lynn. I really can't."

"I didn't cause it. Mia did. If she hadn't opened her big mouth—"

"She did the right thing," Ariel cut her off. "You know it, Jenny."

"The right thing is not to squeal on your friend," Jenny said.

"It is when your friend is doing something she shouldn't," Tristan said quietly, and Jenny blushed.

"Okay. So, maybe it isn't her fault. Maybe it's mine,

but I love Sparkle, and I didn't know he was missing from the training center when I found him. He was just a little baby, and he needed someone to love and care for him. I thought I was doing the right thing."

"Until you heard we were missing a dog and kept him anyway?" Ryder asked, and Jenny's flush deepened.

"I'm sorry. I should have brought him back, but by that time, I already loved him so much." A tear slipped down her cheek and she wiped it away.

"I understand, honey," Ms. Gilmore said, leaning in and giving Jenny a hug.

Jenny sobbed and knelt next to the puppy, pulling him into her arms. The dog licked her cheek, put a paw on her thigh.

"I guess you have to take him," Jenny said morosely, kissing the dog's snout and standing. "He knows all the basic commands, and I've been working with him on puzzles, he's really good at finding anything I hide." Her voice broke, but she seemed determined not to let another tear slip out.

That made the situation even sadder.

At least, to Ariel it did.

Jenny was a tough girl because she'd had to be, but she'd shown a softer side on a few occasions, and she'd obviously done a great job caring for the puppy. He looked healthy and happy, his tongue lolling out as he watched Jenny intently.

"He's going to miss me so much," Jenny whispered, and then she took off, running up stairs that creaked and groaned beneath her light weight.

"I know she's going to have to be punished for this, but it almost seems like giving up the dog is punishment enough," Ms. Gilmore said, shaking her head sadly, the force of the movement loosening her dangling earring. It flew off, clattering onto the floor.

Tristan bent to retrieve it, seemed to freeze as he grabbed the old pearl clip-on.

"We need to get back to the station," he said abruptly, handing Ms. Gilmore the earring and calling for Jesse to heel.

That was it.

No explanation.

He just sprinted out the door and ran toward his SUV.

Ariel was doing her best to rush after him, when he stopped short, turned toward her.

"Sorry about that," he said with a tense smile, returning to take her arm and walk her the rest of the way. Slowly. As if she was fragile and delicate.

That would have made her laugh, if he hadn't looked so upset, his blue eyes shadowed, his jaw tight.

"What's wrong?" she asked, as he opened her door.

"Did that earring remind you of anything?" he asked.

She started to shake her head, then realized that it did. It looked something like the one that had fallen out of Mia's bag. "I guess it does look a little like the one Mia had in her bag. You don't think she stole it, do you? Because it isn't a match to the one Ms. Gilmore was wearing. It looks like it, but it's not the same."

"No. But I know what's been bothering me. I know why every time I see those earrings or see Carrie Dunleavy, I have the feeling I've missed something."

"What—?" she started to ask, but he'd backed away.

She watched as he jogged to Ryder's vehicle, the strobe lights flashing across his face as he said something that Ariel couldn't hear.

Whatever it was got Ryder moving. He lifted the shepherd puppy into the back of the SUV and whistled for his partner who jumped in beside Sparkle.

"I'll meet you back there. Hopefully, Sophie has already arrived. I want the microchip read now," he said, his voice gruff. Then, he was in the SUV and speeding away.

Tristan loaded Jesse into the back of the vehicle, then jumped into the driver's seat.

"Seat belt?" he asked as he started the engine.

"Yes."

That was it.

The sum total of the conversation.

Tristan didn't speak another word as he drove back to the station. He didn't say anything as he helped her from his SUV, then ran to greet Ryder and the puppy, Jesse prancing beside him.

She followed as they walked into the lobby and through the long hallway. She could hear voices. Men and women speaking in hushed tones and in loud ones.

She wasn't sure she should be there, because she could feel the frantic energy in the building, feel the tension that seemed to fill it.

She wanted to suggest that she go home. She could have easily walked, but the thought of Mitch potentially being alive, maybe waiting for her to let down her guard, sealed her lips.

Tristan glanced over his shoulders, met her eyes. "Just give me a few minutes, and I'll take you home," he said as if he'd read her mind.

"Okay," she responded, but he was already moving toward a conference room, the door opened to reveal a crowd of people and dogs.

Chief Jones stood near the doorway, his back to the hall, his hair mussed. He'd been looking tired lately, the unsolved cases taking their toll on him. Ariel had heard the discontented murmurings of more than one Desert Valley resident. The chief of police was being blamed for the fact that Veronica's murder hadn't been solved, and for the fact that the murder of Ryder Hayes's wife was still being investigated five years later. Then there'd been the missing puppy, the attack on Marian Foxcroft and the string of break-ins that had been occurring since the puppy disappeared.

None of those things had been resolved, and Chief Jones was the obvious scapegoat. People were whispering that he should retire, and Ariel was certain he knew about it.

A young woman stood beside him, long blond hair spilling down her back. She held a white wand-like device in one hand, a collar and leash in the other.

The lead dog trainer who'd taken Veronica Earnshaw's place. Sophie Williams. That was her name. Ariel had heard a lot about her from Mia and Jenny. The two girls were fascinated by everything and anyone who had anything to do with dogs.

The trainer must have heard them approaching. She turned, her attention going straight to the puppy.

"Is this Marco?" she asked, crouching and holding out her hand.

"Yes," Tristan responded. "Is Carrie around?" he asked, and Sophie frowned.

"I have no idea. I haven't seen her since I got here. Why?" She attached the collar to the puppy and snapped on the leash. The dog seemed unfazed by the commotion and not in the least bothered by the other dogs that were gathered with their handlers.

"I wanted to speak with her."

"This is the second time you've asked about her, Tristan," Chief Jones said. "What's going on?"

Tristan stared at him. "The pearl earring found in the evidence room near where Veronica Earnshaw's evidence box had been. The matching earring found skittering out of my sister's backpack. I think I've seen those earrings before. He walked into the room and took a photograph from the wall. It looked like a group shot taken at a Christmas party, a bunch of men and women smiling happily at the camera.

Tristan studied it for a moment, then shook his head. "I don't know how I missed it. Look." He jabbed at the photo, his finger touching Carrie's face.

"What?" Ellen said, leaning a little closer, her eyes going wide. "Carrie is wearing the earrings. The exact match for both earrings."

"What?" Chief Jones snatched the photograph from Tristan's hands, his face going pale as he studied it. "No way. There is no way she stole that evidence."

"How else do you explain the earring?" Tristan asked. "She had access to the evidence room. She also had access to my sister's backpack. They hung out here together a couple of times while Mia was waiting for me."

"But…couldn't be it a coincidence?" the chief sputtered, clearly unable to believe the longtime department secretary could be guilty. Of much more than stealing evidence. And planting evidence.

"She probably thought she'd throw us off her trail. You noticed the picture the other day," Shane pointed out. "You said something to me and her about it."

Tristan nodded. "Right. Where is she?"

"Hold on!" the chief growled. "Before we go chasing her down and accusing her. Let's read that microchip."

* * *

Tristan waited impatiently while Sophie scanned the puppy. He didn't need more evidence. He already knew the truth. Carrie was somehow involved in Veronica's murder.

"That's it," Sophie said, eyeing the small screen on the front of the scanner. "Oh boy," she murmured.

"What?" the chief asked, and she turned the scanner so everyone could see it.

Carrie D DVPD.

"We need to find her. Now." Shane Weston headed for the door, brushing past Tristan in his hurry to find Carrie.

Tristan was in a hurry, too, but he couldn't leave Ariel standing around the police department, and he wasn't going to let her return home alone.

He took her arm, leading her out of the conference room that was suddenly filled with people voicing opinions and making plans. He'd be part of that. Eventually.

Right now, Ariel was his priority.

She looked exhausted, her eyes deeply shadowed.

"If you need to stay," she began, and he shook his head.

"It won't take long to get you home and make sure you're safe. I want Jesse with you."

"I really don't mind waiting. It seems like you have a lot of things to work out here."

"We've got a good team. They'll make the plans while I drop you off. We'll follow through on them later."

"What's going to happen to the puppy?" she asked as he backed out of his parking space and headed across town.

"I'm not sure. We'll talk to Sophie, see what she has to say and then make a decision."

"Sophie is the new lead trainer, right?"

"Yes. She took Veronica's place." He didn't mention the

murder. She didn't ask about it. Ariel seemed to understand the boundaries he had, the fact that his job wasn't always something he could discuss.

He liked that about her.

He liked a lot of things about her.

Including her willingness to be there for her students.

"It was nice of you to go out to the Gilmores' place tonight."

"I was just doing my job, Tristan."

"I don't think your job requires late-night visits to students," he responded, and she laughed quietly.

"In a town this size, it does. In Las Vegas, I taught five classes every day. Thirty students in each one. I only got to know most of them on a surface level. Here, I get to know them individually. When you know someone, you can't ignore the troubles they might have. You can't just turn your back and walk away when you know they're hurting."

"Some people can."

"You couldn't," she pointed out, and he knew she was right.

He'd be heading back out to the Gilmores' tomorrow, checking in on Jenny and her grandmother, making sure they were both doing okay. He might even try to help Jenny find a dog she could train and keep, because he was beginning to think Mia was right. Jenny wasn't a bad kid. She just needed a few adults in her life that could steer her in the right direction.

"You're thinking about Jenny, aren't you?" Ariel asked as he pulled onto her street.

"How did you know?"

"Just a guess. I was thinking about her, too. The puppy seems to be doing really well. She did a good job with him. Maybe in addition to volunteering at the K-9 train-

ing center, she could get a little extra training from someone on your team? Someone who might be able to get her
turned on to K-9 training as a career choice."

"By someone, I'm thinking you mean me."

"Someone needs to care, Tristan."

She was right, and he would have told her that, but
Jesse barked, the sound ringing through the vehicle.

Odd, because Jesse almost never barked.

Unless he sensed danger.

"What is it, boy?" Tristan asked, and the dog barked
again, a loud fierce sound that made Tristan's hair stand
on end.

He glanced in the rearview mirror, sure he caught a
hint of movement in the darkness, a shadow darting from
one tree to another.

They were close to the parsonage. Just two houses
down. He could see the lights from her front porch, a
light in the window upstairs.

He kept driving in that direction, pretending he hadn't
seen the guy scurrying through the darkness, but Ariel
sensed the trouble the same way he had, and she twisted
in her seat, her belly brushing his arm as she leaned over
to get a better look.

"What's going on?" she whispered as if she was afraid
whoever was outside might hear her.

"Maybe nothing," he responded, but Jesse growled, the
sound low and mean, the harshness of it a warning that
there *was* something wrong, and that Tristan had better
be prepared for it.

He called his location in on the radio, asking for
backup as he pulled into Ariel's driveway. He knew most
of the rookies would be looking for Carrie Dunleavy, but
at least one of them would respond to Tristan's call. The

area around her house seemed empty, the early morning silence eerie.

Jesse growled again, this time lunging at the back window, his claws scrabbling against the kennel.

"Someone is out there," Ariel said, so quietly he almost didn't hear.

She'd found his hand, holding on as if her life depended on it, her skin cool and dry against his palm.

He didn't think she realized it, but he did, and he squeezed gently, offered her the only reassurance he could.

"It's going to be okay," he said, his attention focused on the porch, the light and what looked like a small string that seemed to hang from it.

A fuse of some sort?

At the end of the street, strobe lights flashed, and he knew his backup had arrived.

"Stay here," he said, opening the door.

"He's out there, Tristan," she replied, holding on to his hand when he would have pulled away. "I know he is."

"Your ex?"

"Who else would hate me and the baby enough to do this?"

"If it is him, I'm going to put a stop to this."

"He knows how to use a gun," she said, and he touched her cheek, looking into her eyes. He wanted to escort her to the house and lock her safely inside, but that string was bothering him. If it had been there before, he'd have noticed.

"I do, too. Shane just pulled up. I need to talk to him. Stay here."

She nodded, finally releasing his hand and offering a halfhearted smile. "Be careful."

He didn't need the warning.

If Mitch really was alive, the guy had nothing to lose and everything to gain by escaping.

He nodded, closed the door and opened the back hatch for Jesse. The dog had barely jumped from the back when he started barking, the loud, sharp warning that said he scented something.

Shane Weston was already out of his vehicle, K-9 partner, Bella, at his side.

"He's alerting?" he asked.

"Yeah."

"Where'd you see the guy?"

"A couple houses to the east."

"I'll head in that direction. Ellen and Whitney are on the way over."

"Ryder?"

"Heading to Carrie's place with James and the chief. Do you really think she murdered Veronica?" he asked.

"How about we handle one problem at a time?" Tristan responded, clipping Jesse to his lead, and then giving the dog the command to find.

The lab took off running, nose to the air, heading straight for the house and that small piece of string that was twisting just a little in the warm summer breeze.

FOURTEEN

There were people everywhere.

Police officers. Bomb squad. Neighbors.

Ariel could see them all from her position in the window of Millie Raymond's house. The older woman had offered to let her sit there while the explosive experts disarmed the bomb that had been left in the porch light fixture.

Mitch's doing?

She had a horrible feeling it was.

Tristan and Shane were out with their K-9 partners, and Ariel needed to remember they were trained for this. They'd find Mitch just as they'd found the thug he'd hired.

She needed to have faith.

"You know what you need, my dear?" Millie said as if reading her mind, her voice a little shaky with age. She'd lost her husband a few years ago, and she'd filled her life with charitable work. She served food at the local mission and rocked babies in the NICU. Apparently, she also took care of terrified neighbors.

Faith, Ariel thought. *That's what I need.* "What?"

"A nice cup of tea. Let's go in the kitchen, and I'll make you some."

Ariel managed a smile. "That's okay, Millie. I'm fine."

"Fine? You've been sitting there for three hours watching the sun come up and all those people run around outside. That can't be good for the baby."

"Tristan said that if I came over here with you, I should stay where he could see me."

"Tristan... Good-looking guy."

"Yes. He is."

"He's also a nice young man. I've seen him over at your house on several occasions."

"It's not my house," she hedged, because she didn't feel like discussing her love life with Millie.

Her love life?

The thought almost made her laugh.

Except that she felt something every time she looked into Tristan's eyes. Something warm and nice and just a little exciting. Something that she should ignore but couldn't seem to.

"You know what I mean, dear. He's been at the parsonage with his sister, helping you out."

"I've been tutoring Mia."

"It will be hard to step into a teenager's life, but I'm sure you're up to the task."

"What are you talking about, Millie. Tutoring her isn't the same as stepping into her life."

"No. It isn't," the older woman said, smiling slyly.

"Whatever you're thinking, stop."

"I'm thinking romance and candles and all the wonderful things a woman your age should have."

"How about I just take a cup of tea instead," Ariel responded, forcing herself to stand. Outside, the sun was just beginning to rise, the first rays of it tingeing the morning with purple light. Across the street, the little parsonage was lit like a Christmas tree, spotlights turned to the porch where several men were working to remove evidence.

There'd been enough explosives to take down the entire house. Tristan had told her that when he'd helped her out of the car and walked her to Whitney's vehicle. He'd wanted her to go to the police station, but Millie had been standing on her front porch watching the action, and she'd offered to bring Ariel inside.

"Just stay where I can see you, okay?" he'd whispered, his lips brushing her hair.

And, she'd told him that she would.

"I've got a wonderful Earl Grey," Millie gushed, leading the way through the small bungalow and into the kitchen. It was at the back of the house, butting up to trees and open land. A pretty property that Millie's husband had bought when they were newlyweds. There were pictures of the life they'd lived together on every wall and every shelf, candid shots and posed ones of the couple growing old together.

Such a nice dream.

One Ariel wished she could still have.

"Do you take cream with your tea? Sugar?" Millie poured hot water into a teacup, dunked a tea bag in it. She had no finesse, but what she lacked in grace, she made up for in enthusiasm. Tea splattered over the rim of the mug as she handed it to Ariel, dropped onto the pristine floor.

"Oh dear!" Millie grabbed a rag. "I'm getting clumsier every day."

"Me, too," Ariel responded, taking the rag from her hand. "I'll do this. You go ahead and make your cup of tea."

"Tea? I'm not pregnant. I'm having soda. High-octane. Which…" she whispered, "means it's caffeinated. A woman my age needs all the help with energy that she can get."

She wobbled over to the fridge, yanked the door open as Ariel bent to clean the floor, her stomach making the task more difficult than it should have been.

She swiped at the drop once. Then again, trying to get to her feet when glass shattered, pieces of the window flying into the room landing near her hands, in her hair, on her skin.

Millie screamed, the sound echoed by a loud pop.

This time a bullet smashed into the wall behind Ariel.

She scrambled away, grabbing Millie's arm and dragging her into the hallway. It was a shotgun-style house, and she could see the front door from there. She could also see the back door, the little windows in the top panel, the man who was peering in.

Mitch! His face, his eyes, everything as familiar as breathing.

He shouted something, the words lost to the frantic gallop of Ariel's heart. Then he stepped back, and she knew what he planned. She shoved Millie forward, covering the older woman as the glass in the door shattered, bits of wood flying into the hallway.

He was coming in, and he didn't care that there were police everywhere, that he was going to be caught, that he might die.

All he cared about was paying Ariel back for whatever it was he thought she'd done. Getting pregnant? Insisting on having the baby?

Surviving when he'd wanted her to die?

She grabbed Millie's hand, dragging her to the door as another bullet slammed into the hallway. She didn't hear the explosion, just felt it, the air charged with her fear and Millie's, the sharp scent of gunpowder mixing with it.

He had to have a silencer on the gun, and she had no

idea if anyone across the street knew he was there, but the door was just ahead, escape within reach.

She grabbed the doorknob and released the bolt with Millie shrieking beside her.

Behind them, the back door flew open, banging against the wall as Mitch barreled into the house.

She shouldn't have looked back. Ariel knew it, but she couldn't help herself. She glanced over her shoulder as she managed to open the front door and shove Millie outside.

And, he was there, his face filled with rage, a gun in his hand.

"You should have listened to me, Ariel," he said, his voice cold. "You should have gotten rid of the baby."

His hand tightened on the gun, and she knew he was going to pull the trigger, knew she'd never make it outside before the bullet flew.

She dived through the front doorway, Millie's squealing shrieks still ringing through the air, the sound of other people shouting, of dogs barking, of Tristan yelling her name filling her ears as she tumbled onto the porch and rolled to try to protect the baby.

A gun.

A silencer.

Mitch.

Tristan could see them all as he raced across the street. Jesse snarled and snapped beside him, and he let the dog go, ordering him to cease, as he aimed for the guy in the front door of the old bungalow, shouted for him to drop his weapon.

Wasn't going to happen.

Tristan knew it.

Mitch was committed to his course, and that course was murder.

Ariel scrambled across the porch, trying desperately to grab Millie's hand and drag her away. They weren't going to make it. Not before Mitch could fire again.

"Drop the weapon," Tristan commanded again.

Mitch ignored him. Ignored the commands of Whitney, Ellen, Ed and Shane.

He raised the weapon, aimed at Ariel.

Tristan fired.

One shot, and it was a good one.

Mitch went down, the gun clattering across the old floorboards and falling onto the ground.

Everyone moved at once. Shane sprinting to the perp's prone body, checking his vitals, shaking his head.

Dead.

Tristan couldn't rejoice in that, but Mitch had gotten what he'd been asking for.

He bypassed the fallen gunman and knelt beside Ariel. She had her arms around Millie murmuring words of comfort, her gaze on Mitch and the blood that was staining the ground near him.

"I'm sorry," Tristan said, touching her chin, forcing her to look in his eyes.

"Don't be," she responded, her voice shaky. "He would have killed me, Tristan. He didn't care if he died doing it."

"Ms. Millie," Whitney said, moving in and putting her arm around the older woman. "Let's get you out of here."

"I can't leave my house," the older woman wailed. "My back door is broken. Someone might walk in and take my valuables."

"Officer Harmon will keep an eye on things here," Whitney assured her. "I promise. Now, how about I drive you to the clinic and have a doctor check you out. Just to make sure you're okay." She led Millie away, and Tristan wrapped an arm around Ariel's waist, helping her to her feet.

"Are you okay?" he asked, his lips brushing her soft hair.

"I think so." She stepped back, ran a hand over her belly, then brushed bits of glass from her hair. She had a tiny cut on her cheek, and he pressed the edge of his sleeve to it.

"You must have been hit by a piece of glass."

"I'm really fortunate I wasn't hit by more than that. I should have stayed at the window. Next time—"

"Let's not have a next time, okay?" he said. "My heart can't take it."

She smiled at that, a shy curving of the lips that made him think of early morning walks and late evening talks.

"Tell you what," she said, leaning on him a little as he led her past Mitch and away from the house. "Let's not have this kind of next time. Let's have something better. Something that doesn't take a few years off each of our lives."

"Like?" he asked, calling to Jesse who ambled over, moping a little because he'd been kept out of the action.

"Breakfast? Or lunch? Or even dinner?" she suggested.

"No teenage sister?" he guessed, and she frowned.

"Of course, teenage sister. And, her friend. Jenny needs some adults in her life who can put her on the right path. I don't see why we can't be that for her."

"We? As in the two of us together. That could lead to something, Ariel. You know that, right?"

"Yes," she said, then smiled again. "I like the idea of that, Tristan. A lot. You remind me of all the dreams I used to have. The ones where some nice guy came along and swept me off my feet and I lived happily ever after. I'm falling for you, but... I've got a lot of baggage to work through, a lot of fears I need to let go of." She glanced back at the house, at Mitch's body now covered by a white sheet, and her smile fell away.

"I didn't want him to die," she said quietly. "But, I'm not sorry that I'm finally free."

"I understand," he said, turning her away from the house again, leading her across the street to his SUV. "And, I'm not going to lie. I'm afraid, too. It's not like I'm winning father of the year with my sister. I don't want to mess things up with your daughter."

"You're doing a great job with Mia," she said, touching his cheek.

"I guess we'll ask her what she thinks in a couple of years." He smiled. "So, we'll take things slow. Maybe we'll find what we're both looking for. How does that sound?"

She looked into his eyes, silent for moment, and then she nodded. "I think that sounds like more than I ever thought I could have."

He lifted her hand, pressed a kiss to her palm and curved her fingers over it. "You're much more than I ever thought I'd have. Keep that in mind, okay? When my sister is going nuts, and I'm going nuts, and life is so crazy that you think I've forgotten about you."

"I will. As long as you keep it in mind when the baby is here, and I'm distracted, and life is crazy, and you wish you'd found someone without all the baggage I'm carrying."

"We make quite the pair, Ariel," he said, and he meant it in the best possible way.

She squeezed his hand, her gaze shifting to a point just beyond his shoulder. "We do—"

"Tristan!" Ryder called, and Tristan glanced over his shoulder and saw his coworker striding toward him.

"What's up?"

"I got a search warrant for Carrie's place."

"That was quick."

"The judge is very aware of what's been going on, and he agreed that we have probable cause." Ryder's gaze shifted, dropping to Ariel's hand. The one Tristan was still holding.

He didn't let go.

He wasn't going to make a secret of his feelings.

"You want me to conduct the search with you?" Tristan asked.

"Chief Jones got the call that things were under control here. He said grab the first K-9 officer I saw. You're it."

"Where is he?" Tristan asked, opening the back hatch of the SUV. Jesse jumped in, settling into the crate with a satisfied sigh.

"Back at the station, fielding questions from a few concerned citizens who heard there was a bomb in town. He's up to his eyeballs in citizen complaints, so I told him we could handle the search."

"Give me five," Tristan requested, and Ryder nodded, striding toward the group working evidence recovery. He turned to face Ariel again. "I'm going to have to go."

"It's okay."

"You should be able to get back in the parsonage soon. Or, I can have Ellen bring you to my place."

"Stop worrying," she said with a smile. "I'm out of danger. The baby is fine, and I think I can handle finding my own ride to wherever I want to go."

"Where would that be?"

"Anywhere you might show up later," she responded, grinning broadly as she turned away. "We still have breakfast, lunch and dinner to do, Tristan. I won't forget if you don't."

He wouldn't, but she didn't give him time to say it.

She walked to the parsonage and started talking to Ellen, offering a quick wave in Tristan's direction.

And, he knew he was lost.

Sunk into that thing he'd never thought he'd feel.

Not just like. Love. The kind that really would last forever.

He got in the SUV, following Ryder over to Carrie's place. The small house wasn't much to look at from the outside. Just a small brick rancher, the lawn green and pretty enough.

Ryder was already at the front door, Bella beside him as he dug through a potted plant.

"Looking for an extra key."

"She keeps one here."

"And, you know this why?"

"She's mentioned it before. I think after my wife was killed." He frowned. "Yeah. That was it. She said that if I ever needed a place to go, somewhere where I wouldn't be reminded of what I'd lost, I could come here and chill. There'd always be a key in the potted plant." He smiled grimly, pulling a key from the dirt. "I guess she wasn't lying."

"You sure she's not home?" Tristan asked, knocking on the door.

"Her car isn't here. There's no garage. We've already put out an APB on her and the car." Ryder shoved the key into the lock. "I don't know about you, but I'm shocked that Carrie is connected to Veronica's death. But the microchip points to her for a reason. She stole the box of evidence on Veronica's murder for a reason. She has to be guilty."

"I'm as shocked as you are," Tristan responded, walking into a small sparsely furnished living room. "But why kill Veronica? What was her motive?"

"No clue," Ryder added. "But now I know why she

was always around when anyone needed anything—she was keeping tabs on us."

"Always around *period*," Tristan said, pulling on a pair of disposable gloves and lifting the couch cushions. Not even a crumb was hidden beneath them. "How about we start in a room visitors normally wouldn't see?" Ryder suggested. "We can work our way to the front rooms."

They headed down a narrow hall. No photos. No pictures. Nothing to give any hint of who Carrie really was.

The first room to the left was her bedroom, the frilly bedspread and drapes a pale pink that even Mia would have turned her nose up at. They looked through drawers, lifted the mattress, hunted under the bed. Everything was neat and organized, devoid of any hint into Carrie's personality.

They did the same in a spare bedroom, then walked to the end of the hall and tried the door there.

"Locked," Tristan said, wiggling the knob a second time. "Wonder why?"

"Let's find out." Ryder jimmied the lock and pushed open the door. The room smelled like rotten rose petals, the air thick and musty.

"What is that stench?" Tristan muttered, feeling for the wall switch and turning on the light.

It wasn't a white light.

No. This one was pink, the weird glow barely illuminating the room. Heavy drapes were pulled across a lone window, and one piece of furniture stood against the far wall.

A bench?

Table?

Tristan walked into the room, wrinkling his nose at the cloying scent of dead flowers. Jesse growled, his hackles raised. Apparently, he didn't like it, either.

"What is that?" Ryder said, the tension in his voice matching what Tristan was feeling.

There was something really off about this.

He approached the table, realizing there were photos on it and on the wall beyond it. Photos of people.

No. A person.

Photos of…

He glanced at Ryder, his colleague's expression one of shock—and horror. Almost every picture on the wall was of Ryder. Smiling. Frowning. Standing with his wife, her face cut out of the photo.

"She did it," Ryder said, the words hoarse, his voice tight. "She killed my wife."

"You don't know that," Tristan said, but the proof was staring them in the face. Or, at least, the evidence that it might be true. Every photo of Ryder and his wife had Melanie cut out. There were other photos, too, and Tristan lifted one, studying it carefully.

Mike. Standing in a group of people. Only someone had drawn a red X through his face. Brian Miller was in another picture, his face crossed out, too. A photo of Veronica lay on the floor, the same red X through her face.

"She was nuts," Ryder muttered.

"She *is* nuts," Tristan corrected. "Now that we know it, we can stop her."

"From what? Killing again? Because based on what I'm seeing here, we've already let her get away with four murders."

"Right, and I think we can also say," Tristan responded, lifting one of the many photos of Ryder, "that you might be her next target."

"Forewarned is forearmed," Ryder growled, then he turned on his heel and stalked from the room. "I'm calling the chief. We need some more manpower here. We've got a lot of evidence to collect."

And a lot of ground to cover if they were going to find Carrie and stop her before she could strike again.

Tristan set the photos down, took out his phone and started snapping pictures, documenting the shrine that Carrie had created. A shrine to a man that she'd loved so obsessively, she'd been willing to commit murder to have him.

The team would gather to discuss Carrie's murder trail, but Tristan was sure she'd murdered Ryder's wife, Melanie. She'd murdered the rookies. She'd murdered Veronica Earnshaw. And she'd attacked Marian Foxcroft. What Tristan wasn't sure of was the connections—Melanie's murder made sense, given Carrie's obsession with her husband, Ryder. But how did that lead to Mike Riverton's murder? To Brian Miller's? To Veronica's? Why had she attacked Marian?

For those answers, they had to find Carrie. They'd already turned the town upside down. They'd searched every alley, looked in every empty building. So far, they'd come up empty. Tristan didn't want to think that she'd escaped, but he had the sinking feeling she was far away from Desert Valley.

It didn't matter.

They'd hunt her down. No matter how far she'd gone.

FIFTEEN

Three weeks after Carrie had disappeared, and the town was still talking about the manhunt for her.

Ariel tried not to worry about it. She tried not to think of how hard Tristan and the K-9 team were working. Long days, long nights. Tristan looked exhausted, and she wanted nothing more than to see him finally solve the cases that had been haunting him for months.

She sighed, trying to keep a cheerful smile in place. The youth group at the church had planned a baby shower for her, and the kids would be upset if she looked as worried as she felt.

Balloons hung from the rafter of the church's fellowship hall. Pink streamers decorated the windowsills, and a huge white cake with bright pink icing sat in the middle of a table at the front of the room. A dozen smaller tables were spread throughout the large area, covered with plastic tablecloths and silver-and-pink glitter. Pink-and-white mints sat in tiny bowls, and daisies poked up from jelly jars. The flowers, more than anything, made Ariel smile as she sat and watched a bunch of teens play a game that involved changing a doll's clothes and diaper.

The fastest would win the grand prize.

Which was apparently a night babysitting Ariel's daughter.

That had made her laugh.

It seemed every teenager in the church was eager to help out. Most here were students, and they'd insisted on throwing her a baby shower. With the help of the social committee, they'd pulled it off.

In wonderful, wacky teenage style.

Even with the baby kicking and wiggling and keeping her awake at night, Ariel felt good. Soon, her daughter would arrive, and she'd begin her life as a mother. She'd set up the nursery in the parsonage, painting the walls and trim a pretty butter yellow and a bright crisp white.

At night, when nightmares woke her, she'd walk into the room and think about the years to come. All the good things that would eventually overshadow the bad.

It would take time, but eventually the image of Mitch staring at her through the glass in Millie's door would fade. She'd be left with little of the bad and a whole lot of the good.

Like Mia and the way she'd blossomed, accomplishing more academically in a few short weeks than most kids did in months. Mia had been making friends, too. Lots of them. Now that her secret was out, now that she no longer had something weighing on her heart, her true nature was coming out, and the other kids were responding.

Jenny had changed, too. She'd become happier, kinder, more responsible. She'd apologized to the police department for keeping the puppy, and she'd even visited Marian Foxcroft in the hospital, apologizing for taking the pup who Marian had donated to the center. According to Ellen, the teen had promised to volunteer at the center, work hard and pay the training center for whatever the lost puppy had cost.

No one wanted her to do that, of course.

The apology had been enough, and the puppy had been

so well trained, so well socialized and healthy, that Ellen had gifted the puppy to Jenny. Sophie was helping Jenny train Sparkle, and teaching her a few tricks of the trade. That had given Jenny something to work toward, something to be proud of. That had shown itself in her schoolwork. It hadn't improved as much as Mia's, but she'd passed her summer courses and would enter tenth grade in a few weeks.

Both girls were excited about that. Summer school had ended a week ago, but Mia and Jenny visited Ariel often, stopping by the house with tales of their dog-training adventures, plans for their tenth grade year and lots of girlish giggles.

And, then, of course, there was Tristan.

Having him in her life was the biggest surprise and the biggest blessing Ariel had ever received.

As if her thoughts had conjured him, Tristan walked into the room, Jesse trotting along beside him. They'd been working, and Tristan was in his crisp blue uniform, Jesse wearing his work harness. They made a handsome pair and Ariel wasn't ashamed to admit she noticed.

She'd also noticed just how hard the two had been working recently. Hour after hour chasing down leads, trying to stop Carrie before she struck again. Despite the best efforts of the Desert Valley PD, the secretary hadn't been found. She'd apparently gone deep into hiding, and everyone on the force was working overtime trying to find her. There'd been little information released about her, little said to the public, but rumors were rampant. People whispering about obsessive love, murder, a secret shrine. Someone who worked on the police force had said that Carrie had been completely enamored of Ryder, and that she'd have done anything to have him.

Ariel was pretty sure the one who'd been spreading

the rumors was Eddie Harmon. He'd been inside Carrie's house. He'd seen what she'd been hiding. And he liked to talk almost as much as he liked to spend time with his family.

Ariel hadn't mentioned the rumors to Tristan. She was sure he'd already heard them.

She also hadn't joined in the gossip, and she didn't ask Tristan to tell her more than he'd been able to. He didn't need that kind of pressure, and she cared too much to burden him with her own curiosity or the curiosity of others.

He did look tired, though—his eyes shadowed and a day's worth of stubble on his jaw—and that worried her.

"You look happy," he said, leaning in and offering her a sweet kiss that made her toes curl and her heart sing.

"I am. This is more than I could ever have hoped for."

"You hoped for less than pink glitter and baby-changing games?" he teased, picking up a handful of gaudy faux gems that one of the girls had tossed on the table.

"I just hoped for peace," she said seriously, because she wouldn't ever downplay how much he meant to her, how much this new beginning meant. "And I got joy and happiness and friendship. And love. That's a lot, Tristan, and I'm so thankful for it."

He smiled gently. "I'm thankful for you. You're a little bit of sanity in my crazy world. Sometimes I need that way more than I'm willing to admit."

"Rough workday?" she asked, taking his hand and pulling him into the chair beside her.

"Sad workday. The more we learn about Carrie..." He shook his head. "Let's just say that it's rough for all of us, but especially for Ryder."

"I wish there was something I could do, some way I could help."

"You're helping by being here." He tucked a strand

of hair behind her ears, his fingers skimming across her skin. "By being you. I still can't believe how fortunate I am. I came here thinking I'd go through training and go home. God had bigger plans than that. Better ones."

"Eventually you'll find Carrie. When that happens, will you stay in Desert Valley?" She hoped he would, because she loved the little town, but if he left, she thought that she'd leave, too. Wherever Tristan and Mia were, that's where she wanted to be.

"That depends," he responded, his gaze on his sister. Mia was frantically yanking clothes off a doll, her hair pulled back, her face wreathed in a smile. She was laughing so hard, she could barely get a diaper from a package on the table.

"On Mia?" Ariel asked, because she thought that the teenager was doing well, but she could understand if Tristan decided that returning to Phoenix would be best for Mia. He'd made a promise when they'd come for his training, and she knew he didn't want to break it.

"Mia is happy. She told me that she wants to stay here forever." He turned his attention back to Ariel, and she looked into his dark eyes, saw the future there, written in the love that shone from the depth of his soul. "Whether I stay depends on you, Ariel. Mia and I both want to be wherever you are. We've talked about it, and we agreed. She wants to be a big sister, and I want to be a father, a husband, a best friend. I know I'm not going to be perfect at it, but I hope you'll give me the chance to try. Love isn't about one moment, right? It's about all the moments added together to make a beautiful life. I want that with you. Every moment. The good ones and the bad ones."

He took something from his pocket, and her heart jumped, her pulse raced and all the noise from the teenagers and the church ladies faded as Tristan opened a small box and took a ring from it.

"This was my mother's ring. I was talking about getting you one, and Mia suggested it. She said that I should make my proposal romantic, but I'm not that kind of guy. Besides, the baby could come any day, and when she's older, I want to say I was her father from the very beginning. Will you marry me, Ariel?"

She nodded, her hand shaking as he slipped the ring on.

She hadn't expected to find love again, but maybe she'd never had it the first time, because the way she felt with Tristan? It was like every dream she'd ever had coming true, every blessing she'd ever longed for being handed to her.

She didn't realize she was crying until he wiped a tear from her cheek.

"Happy tears?" he asked.

"Happy for what I have. Sad because I wasted so much time finding it."

"No, you didn't," he whispered as he leaned in and kissed her tenderly. "You got here just at the right time to meet me and Mia, to touch our lives, to steal my heart. I promise I will never betray you, I will never lie to you and I will always love your daughter just as much as I love the children we will have together."

"*Our* daughter," she murmured against his lips, and she felt him smile, heard someone clapping. Softly at first, and then more loudly as the teens realized what had happened, and the church ladies rushed to tell the world, and everything Ariel had ever wanted was suddenly hers.

* * * * *

If you liked this ROOKIE K-9 UNIT *novel,*
watch for the thrilling conclusion to the series,
SEARCH AND RESCUE *by Valerie Hansen.*

Dear Reader,

I hope you've been enjoying the exciting Rookie K-9 series! I've been so blessed to be part of it and to work with a great team of authors and editors. As I wrote Ariel and Tristan's story I was reminded of how important family is, of how we so often long for the connections that tie us together. Husband to wife. Children to parents. Brothers to sisters. These are God-given relationships, and they are meant to be valued and cherished. May God bless you and your family and help you build bonds that will stand the test of time.

I love to hear from readers. If you have the time, drop me a line at shirlee@shirleemccoy.com.

Blessings,

Shirlee McCoy

LISCNM0816

REQUEST YOUR FREE BOOKS!
2 FREE RIVETING INSPIRATIONAL NOVELS PLUS 2 FREE MYSTERY GIFTS

Love Inspired.
SUSPENSE
RIVETING INSPIRATIONAL ROMANCE

YES! Please send me 2 FREE Love Inspired® Suspense novels and my 2 FREE mystery gifts (gifts are worth about $10). After receiving them, if I don't wish to receive any more books, I can return the shipping statement marked "cancel." If I don't cancel, I will receive 4 brand-new novels every month and be billed just $4.99 per book in the U.S. or $5.49 per book in Canada. That's a savings of at least 17% off the cover price. It's quite a bargain! Shipping and handling is just 50¢ per book in the U.S. and 75¢ per book in Canada.* I understand that accepting the 2 free books and gifts places me under no obligation to buy anything. I can always return a shipment and cancel at any time. Even if I never buy another book, the two free books and gifts are mine to keep forever.

123/323 IDN GH5Z

Name	(PLEASE PRINT)	
Address		Apt. #
City	State/Prov.	Zip/Postal Code

Signature (if under 18, a parent or guardian must sign)

Mail to the **Reader Service**:
IN U.S.A.: P.O. Box 1867, Buffalo, NY 14240-1867
IN CANADA: P.O. Box 609, Fort Erie, Ontario L2A 5X3

Are you a current subscriber to Love Inspired® Suspense books and want to receive the larger-print edition?
Call 1-800-873-8635 or visit www.ReaderService.com.

LIS15

"I'm going to make a quick run to town and back," Sophie told newly minted police chief Ryder Hayes and noted his scowl in response.

"Be careful. You may have been a cop once," Ryder said, "but you're a dog trainer now."

That was a low blow. Sophie clenched her jaw.

"We all have to be on guard," he said. "There's no telling where Carrie is or whether she's through killing people."

"I agree with you. I'll keep my eyes open," Sophie said.

He arched a brow. "Are you carrying?"

"Of course." She patted a flat holster clipped inside the waist of her jeans. "I won't be out and about for long. I'm going to the train station to pick up a dog."

"Why didn't you say so in the first place?"

She was still smiling a few minutes later when she parked at the small railroad station and climbed out of her official K-9 SUV.

A sparse crowd was beginning to disembark as she approached. She shaded her eyes. *There!* A slim young police cadet had stepped down and turned, tugging on a leash. "Hello! I've been expecting you. I'm Sophie Williams."

"This is Phoenix," the young man said, indicating the silver, black and white Australian shepherd cowering at his feet. "I hope you have better success with him than we did."

She grasped the end of the leash, gave it slack and took several steps back. She politely bade him goodbye, turned and walked away with Phoenix at her side.

"Heel," Sophie ordered.

The dog refused to budge.

She faced him. "What is it, boy? What's scaring you?"

A loud bang echoed a fraction of a second later. Sophie recognized a rifle shot and instinctively ducked.

The dog surged toward her. She opened her arms to accept him just as a second shot was fired. Together they scrambled for safety behind her SUV.

Don't miss
SEARCH AND RESCUE by Valerie Hansen,
available wherever
Love Inspired® Suspense books and ebooks are sold.

www.LoveInspired.com

SPECIAL EXCERPT FROM

Love Inspired®

*When Esther Stoltzfus's childhood crush,
Nathaniel Zook, returns to their Amish community
and asks for help with his farm—and an orphaned
boy in need—will their friendship blossom
into a happily-ever-after?*

*Read on for a sneak preview of
HIS AMISH SWEETHEART by Jo Ann Brown,
available September 2016 from Love Inspired!*

"Are you sure you want Jacob to stay with you?" Esther asked.

"I'm sure staying at my farm is best for him now," Nathaniel said. "The boy needs something to do to get his mind off the situation, and the alpacas can help."

Nathaniel held his hand out to assist Esther onto the seat of the buggy.

She regarded him with surprise, and he had to fight not to smile. Her reaction reminded him of Esther the Pester from their childhood, who'd always asserted she could do anything the older boys did...and all by herself.

Despite that, she accepted his help. The scent of her shampoo lingered in his senses. He was tempted to hold on to her soft fingers, but he released them as soon as she was sitting. He was too aware of the *kinder* and other women gathered behind her.

She picked up the reins and leaned toward him. "If it becomes too difficult for you, bring him to our house."

LIEXP0816

"We'll be fine." At that moment, he meant it. When her bright blue eyes were close to his, he couldn't imagine being anything but fine.

Then she looked away, and the moment was over. She slapped the reins and drove the wagon toward the road. He watched it go. A sudden shiver ran along him. The breeze was damp and chilly, something he hadn't noticed while gazing into Esther's pretty eyes.

The sound of the rattling wagon vanished in the distance, and he turned to see Jacob standing by the fence, his fingers through the chicken wire again in the hope an alpaca would come to him. The *kind* had no idea of what could lie ahead for him.

Take him into Your hands, Lord. He's going to need Your comfort in the days to come. Make him strong to face what the future brings, but let him be weak enough to accept help from us.

Taking a deep breath, Nathaniel walked toward the boy. He'd agreed to take care of Jacob and offer him a haven at the farm. Now he had to prove he could.

Don't miss
HIS AMISH SWEETHEART *by Jo Ann Brown,*
available September 2016 wherever
Love Inspired® *books and ebooks are sold.*

www.LoveInspired.com

LIEXP0816